DEAR DIARY
VISIONS OF LOVE LOST& FOUND

S.A. WILLIS

Dear Diary – Visions of Love Lost & Found

Copyright © 2016 S.A. Willis
Cover design © 2014 by Create Space Amazon
Edit by K.B. Stevenson & S.A. Willis

This is a work of non-fiction. Names, characters, places and incidents are the product of the author's work.

ISBN-13: 978-0692285176

Dedication

This book is dedicated to young women, who have or waiting to travel the same road I did in order to find love. Of course, this is all, after we go through the stages of hating boys and calling them losers, because in later years, that's what some of them will be - **LOSERS**.

In true prospective as women, we wait for our Prince Charming to one day appear and to change our lives and show us that fun side of having a boyfriend – yeah a boyfriend, sounds nice huh but the lifestyle with having one is very challenging. Cause for one we have to expose emotions that were hidden away. Like most teenagers, I dreamed of finding that one guy to love and brag about to my friends – during the locker talks and phone conversations.

First, let's begin with those dreaded hormones, that take complete control over your body. Next, you begin to take better care of yourself by dressing and looking cuter for your peers, letting them know what time it is, "wow the memories". Finally, you begin to let your mind cloud all of the good judgment your parents tried to put in you, as if.

One of the things I remembered in middle and high school, was when he would walk me to class while carry my books; or we just sit on the phone till 2 in the morning, talking about nothing.

Dear Diary

Next, when it's time to hang up the phone, you make replies like; "You hang up first. "No you hang up first. "Okay on three we both hang up." Now, you know damn well you don't want to the call the end. Ah, the memories of being young and free; you can only experience these feeling once in a lifetime, but it will take a couple times before you get it right.

The main thing about us has to deal with is what is happening with our bodies. First, let's start off with our raging hormones; which can completely drive you crazy because you're hitting puberty. Next, you begin to take better care of yourself by dressing and looking cute for your peers and letting them know what time it is, "wow the memories". Finally, you begin to let your mind cloud all good judgment your parents tried to put in you, because at this state you know it all. How many times have you said, "I know what I'm doing" when in reality you don't? It's all part of growing up I know this, but sometimes we have to really just listen.

My story consists of all those wonderful memories the people in this book have placed in my heart and mind to share with you.

Content

Chapter 1 — *Hello Young World*

Chapter 2 — *Date Night*

Chapter 3 — *Feeling Crazy*

Chapter 4 — *Valentine's Day*

Chapter 5 — *Phone Sex*

Chapter 6 — *Sharing Each Other*

Chapter 7 — *Bye-Bye Girl*

Chapter 8 — *Leaving Robert*

Chapter 9 — *Living in between*

Chapter 10 — *Being Wild & Free*

Chapter 11 — *Rules to live by*

Chapter 12 — *Finding Malcolm*

Chapter 13 — *The Waiting is over*

Chapter 14 — *Missing my Friend*

Chapter 15 — *Love at Last*

Chapter 16 — *I's Married now*

Introduction

During part of my teen and young-adult life, I sat at home and wrote in a diary my Mom brought me on my fifteenth birthday. She wanted me to open my mind into writing my feelings down, because I was too shy and uptight to express them openly. The only problem was the journals weren't suitable for her eyes.

My long history of love lost was a series of thoughts and events that took place my life. I expressed, categorizes daily events and experiences that flow with what or how I was feeling at the time. Maybe, reminiscing on my life will bring a special memory or feeling that you experienced.

Writing everything out kept the memory alive inside of me. I'm sort of scared over the reaction once it's published, but like I said; my experiences were typical of most teenagers at that age. I wanted to share a part of that with you. It was fun reading & writing this book - but it also let me know I was crazy for living that life too. I was drawn into wanting someone to love me, and not thinking of the pros & cons to the process of having it.

The entries from my diaries are authentic - I didn't want to change anything off course from what was written during that time. So excuse the language and grammar because everything in my journals was raw and real nothing was changed. Beside, at that age I wasn't concerned about anything - I just wanted to get my thoughts down.

While reading this, keep in mind I was 15 and very hot in the ass.

I changed the names in this book to protect the people anonymity and myself.

CHAPTER 1

Hello Young World

It's 1989, the year of high top fades, stone wash denim jeans, bold bright colors and my favorite R&B groups, New Edition, with "NE Heartbreak", and Karyn White talking about not being a "Super Woman", those were the joints. I was fifteen, in the 10th grade, living in a small town called Attapulgus Ga. It's a very rural area with tons of cornfields and sugar cane barns from yester years. I lived with my mom and sister next my dear grandma and a few cousins nearby, down a long red clay dirt road. I had a few relatives in the next town that I loved to visit in Bainbridge. Tonya, my cousin stayed near my high school in Bainbridge, it's located close to all the local shopping area. We had a general hospital, a small mall etc. it was mainly for the surrounding small towns like where I'm from Attapulgus; WOW Attapulgus. Attapulgus had one signal light that only flash either red or yellow a general Mom and pop grocery store, post office, small bank, and an elementary school that I attended up to 6th grade and finally a family owned restaurant for the local mining company. I thought we were something, but Bainbridge was where all the main action occurred. My cousin's house was walking distance from the high school and the bonus was she's family. I never had any idea how small we were, until I venture out to other cities like Tallahassee, Florida.

Throughout my childhood, I didn't have many sleep-over like most of my friends did. The only one I can remember, was at my classmate's house and that was because our moms knew each other, how lame is that. I felt sheltered as a child, kept away from things that seem normal to others, like watching music videos, hanging out after school etc., this kind of explain the party girl effect later in my life. I never really had a boyfriend or even someone take interest in me, for that matter. I felt like an outcast at times, not wearing the latest outfits, stylish hairstyle etc.., it's something we all lack at one point of our lives.

I was a very shy girl trying to fit in; skinny tall with no breasts or ass in sight. In middle school most girls experienced that awkward stage where their body begin to develop with the hormones driving your insides crazy; oh yeah, that was all me from the beginning, I did whatever to fit in except have early sex. I was so frightening about having sex due to the high pregnancy rate in our county; it was crazy to see someone you went to Elementary school with expecting their first child in the 7th grade. I saw a lot of that during my middle school years. It seems like if you kiss a boy BAM, your pregnant. I didn't understand what was happening or why the kids couldn't just wait a while, like "Janet Jackson's song", beside after having to watch and raise my sister who was 10 years younger, was enough baby practice for me. It would of being simple to just say no or put a rubber on, but most times the girls either were pressured into it by their peers or some horny ass little boy. Now in days, it's normal to see a girl pregnant, it's amazing how times have changed, especially values.

I tried to find my way during puberty, but nothing happened until I entered high school and somehow I blossomed into this cute girl, "isn't that something", it's like over the summer milk did my body some good, lol.

When I entered high school it seems like a lot of guys were checking me out, which had me feeling myself. It was exciting being notice, but the weird part was I only flirted with guys but never participated in any sexual activities. I still felt weary about that part, especially with the reputation some girls got, my attractions to the guys were limited to seniors yes SENIORS. I was this freshman that only wanted check out the class of 1988 guys. My cousin, made it easy to meet them because he was a senior. His friends were my playground, with my innocent personality and awesome smile, who could turn me down. I was just a FLIRT plain and simple.

There was a time my flirting almost turned into the real thing. It was a school event that I went too w/ my cousin and friends. I was checking out who was there and notice Lufo there. He was this guy that I thought was extremely cute and of course he was a senior and I wanted to so desperately to get his attention so I took my fast ass to him and just went for it, not knowing the next few minutes' will would've been the end of my innocence's. Lufo invited me into his vehicle which was parked near-by, I said "sure", not knowing he wanted more than conversation. We entered the vehicle and just stared at one another and then suddenly he started kissing and caressing me in places I wasn't expecting surprisingly I became aroused and wanted more but then he pulled out his penis and OMG I somehow became frighten over the sight of it, going from seeing a penis in the magazine to looking at a real one was a shocker for me. I pulled my dress down and jetted out of his car with his penis expose and left him there. That traumatize me a lot, problem was my cousin saw me leave his and assume the worse. Never did I expect that kind of reaction from viewing my first penis, but there you have it.

CHAPTER 2

Date Night

Denise my friend wanted to hook me up with a guy that she felt was boyfriend material. Denise felt it was necessary for me "to open my heart to the possibilities" as she put it. Since I was new with talking to boys and didn't have much of a life at the moment, I was like "What the hell", so I told her; "sure give him the digits and we'll see what happens". So I began this secret relationship with a boy from another school, Denise told me he was a nice guy that had just gotten out of a relationship and was looking for a fresh start. She told me he was 14 and I thought its fine he's younger than me just hope he's mature. Denise told Robert about me, and he wanted to know me better. Robert called me maybe a few days after getting my number and of course I was shock. Like I mentioned earlier, I wasn't experience in the boy's department so getting a call from him was a new first for me. Denise told me to expect his call that evening, but once I got the call I didn't know what to expect but after listening for a few minutes his voice was sort of hypnotizing, I felt calm and relax talking to him, as if we have known each other for years.

I found out Robert was attending high school in Quincy and was a track star there along with being a part time singer @ his church. We talked about his family and mine just really getting to know one another, it was amazing that I could have a conversation with someone, especially a boy for over 2 hours maybe even longer if my mom didn't catch me on the phone. It was refreshing talking to Robert, in fact it was only right to meet up face to face, and really get things started. Since our home football game was next Friday, I thought that would be the perfect place to meet up.

Robert and I, begin planning and making preparations for our mini date. While all this was happening, I never considered if my Mom would even allow me to go. Oh yeah, I forgot to mention; somewhere with getting so consumed with your new relationship, your parents and everyone around you are invisible, **remember it's your world**. At this point, I had to do some convincing to make this whole thing happen, because I was really looking forward to seeing Robert. So I did the basic stuff to make her happy by cleaning up the house, staying on my best behavior and then bust out the question. I had to pick the right moment to throw this at her, or it would look like I planned it. Wednesday evening after we ate dinner (which I prepared, some macaroni cheese, corn bread and some collard greens and my famous cherry flavored cool-aid) ma was in a good mood, so while I was cleaning the kitchen, I decided what the hell, "Ma can I spend the night at Tonya's house this weekend".

Robert and I were still planning our meet n greet day, and with each passing day I was getting more and more nervous about seeing him. All kinds of thoughts were running in my head like what will he think of me, am I cute, ugly or what. I didn't have much self-esteem, and I didn't have anyone around to tell me otherwise. I couldn't believe how insecure I was feeling even after all the big talk I was doing on the phone a few nights before.

Well its Friday, I packed my overnight bag for my mom to drop off at my Aunts. I was on cloud nine the whole day at school; nothing could bring me down, the teachers, dumb boys or my silly friends with suggestions of skipping 6th period to watch the football players during practice. I spoke to my cousin during lunch expressing my excitement with spending the night over her house and going to the game to meet Robert. This was going to the last home game of the season and they were expecting a big crowd since they were going for the National Championship. Friday was finally here and I was getting very anxious throughout the day just waiting for it to end. Mom had already dropped my stuff off earlier before heading to her night job, so I was able to do a quick change and fix myself up before the big game. I told Tonya about Robert and about our plans to meet up, she wanted me to be careful and stay in the crowd, and I didn't understand why since she was meeting with her friends anyway. I told her I'll be safe and we agreed to meet up afterwards, which was cool. Robert and I agreed to wear something so we could find each other. Denise was with me, so there shouldn't be any problems.

Once everything was all good at the home front, Tonya and I left with a few friends; we arrived at the game just in time. I was hyped to see Denise so I left my cousin without saying "see ya". Denise told me how cute I looked and not to be so nervous. She asked me, was I ready to see Robert, and I told her "sure please, before I back out" that's how nervous I was. Instead of focusing on the game I was more into finding out how he looked. Near the 2nd Quarter she started nudging me "there he is" we saw him walking around the field toward the bleachers; my heart was beating 100 mph, my stomach was turning, OMG he's coming. Finally, Denise says "Robert this is Terri Williams, "Terri here is Robert Thomas". I'm like, "finally hi", and of course he laughed and we begin to walk around and just talk all awhile he was checking me out like, "OKAY I see what I'm working with here," "you're cute", 'thanks', I responded with this crazy grin going on, 'like wow he called me cute' it's funny hearing someone call me that other than family. Robert was a cutie himself; he had beautiful brown eyes and an awesome voice that could melt any girl's heart. He was a little shorter than me but why complain. I felt like Cinderella finally meeting her Prince Charming, but if only the night could go on. Instead it ended @ 10:45 PM, LOL. We felt a connection that night, which brings me to all these little entries I've written down. I didn't get this diary until after Christmas so that is where my note taking begins on Feb 10, 1989.

CHAPTER 3

Feeling Crazy
Feb 10, 1989 Friday
Dear Diary,

Today was an ok day, school was over and it was Friday so why complaint. Mom was in good spirits because she got her income tax check and wanted to go shopping in Bainbridge this was a rare experience since money was always tight, but not today. I was supposed to attend the Bearcats game on Friday for their Tri-State Championship, but unfortunately I didn't go because Mom didn't want to pick me up afterward ugh especially after going to Bainbridge earlier, it sucks not having a car or even driver licenses for that matter; but I was able to get some pretty fly clothes to wear next week. Along with a hair do courtesy of mom, she booked a hair appointment for a wash n curl, I wasn't expecting that, but I was happy. After coming home and putting away my clothes, I checked the voice mail and realize Robert hadn't called yet; at that point my mood became bland to the fact that Valentine's Day was coming up soon. Robert the guy I like very much has been hiding something from me. I can't explain the reason for feeling this way, maybe my insecurities were coming not sure.

Our relationship is so fresh and I'm still not sure if he loves me, but the big question in the back of mind is how I would know! Robert finally called and we talked on the phone from 8 p.m. to

9:28 p.m. and of course he felled asleep on me, I knew he had a busy day @ school, but really not feeling up to talking to me, so I ended the conversation because it was getting boring. I really think he's the best guy I've been with; "wait who I am kidding" he's the only guy I've been with. Anyway, this turn out to be one of those "I'm just glad it's over days".

Feb 11, 1989 Saturday
Dear Diary,

Well today started off all right for me I woke up around 9:30 AM to catch the last of The Smurfs and fix a bowl of Count Chocula cereal and watch Pee-Wee's Playhouse (now that was the show) in 89 to 91. Later on I was able to finish my chores before Mom could say anything to me and then after lunch I was able to call this guy name Ronnie I once talk to a year ago.

We tried to have a relationship but things didn't work out so well for us, one he was a total uppity guy, and he was a little boring, but I was willing to give it another try. I wasn't the most popular or the prettiest girl he's ever met, but I was interested in him. I called my friend Fred a fellow class mate to discuss fixing me and Ronnie up again and, when I called him Fred sounded like a grown ass man on the phone then at school I almost hung up the phone. After learning nothing much has change with Mr. Ronnie, I ended the conversation and wind up not doing anything, but looking at a program on TV and ignoring my sister, in meaning it was a boring ass day.

Feb 13, 1989 Monday
Dear Diary,

Today came out to be an okay day. A couple of girlfriends and I went to the local mall to just do some browsing, and all this happened during our lunch break from school. Wow, we were good to get back in time before our next class. In school, my English teacher Mrs. Penhallegon (old witch) called my name for a question, and I answered it correctly, but then she got smart and made the class laugh at me. Later in class Kinsey (he's the type of guy that will fuck anything that comes his way, ole' horny bastard) gave me a note saying, "I want you badly." He's such a liar. After class I finally witnessed Anthony Carter get the "shame on" (it's when a person gets clowned on in front of others) from someone. He's the guy that tried to like me, but I wasn't interested at all, so there was a girl he was trying to hit on, but she completely blew him off, and everyone was tripping over it.

I really never understood the whole fronting thing; it's sort of childish, but that's boys. I was eager to get home to talk with my baby who finally called during our conversation he kept mentioning his brother Cameron wanted to talk to my cousin Tonya, but she knew better besides she had a boyfriend. As we talked I was beginning to realize that somehow I was falling in love with this guy and then another part of me don't it's so confusing.

Robert is so nice and stuff and I'm so crazy about him even though it took 5 months to get with him physically, but somehow I still don't have him emotionally which bothers me more. Robert has been telling me for over a month that he wants to come over but I never told Mama about him, and that fact he wants to here; that's a storm I'm not ready to see. I wanted to ask mama about it but I wasn't sure of her answer, or how she would behave since again no permission was given for me to date, so other than that today was okay for me. We will see what tomorrow brings.

CHAPTER 4

Valentine's Day
Feb 14, 1989 Tuesday
Dear Diary,

To begin my day started and ended in pure hell for me. This morning I woke up thinking about Robert and if he was going to buy me anything or come see me, but screw that let me tell you about school. First, after coming to school with my red sweater and blue jeans trying to fit in with the festivities, I got a High School attendance award and most of the school was in the lunch room. My cousin Tonya didn't come to school; she wasn't feeling well. I wanted to hear about her telephone conversation with Cameron Robert's brother, for the past few months he has been howling me about getting her number.

During school, I saw most of the girls carrying balloons, candy boxes, teddy bears basically painted in Red-n-White. I wanted to experience Valentine once in my miserable life, to have someone come to the class and present me with a Happy Valentine's Day balloon, with a box of chocolates on the side, but it never happened of course, but I have to remember the bigger picture TONIGHT, I'm hoping to see Robert later.

After arriving home excited about my evening with Robert, he called and said, "I'll try to come over there, Cameron is taking his time getting ready", so I put on my neatest clothes and fix my hair and waited, after maybe an hour or so I just assume he wasn't going to show, it hurt so bad inside to think, "not again"! So after crying and throwing things in my room, I pulled up the nerves together and called him. Robert was still coming, but I couldn't understand why a phone call didn't happen, instead having me completely upset over here.

Finally, he told me his brother ended up having other plans and didn't feel like bringing him. Robert asked his dad to bring him over, but I never received an answer from that. I not only wanted him for Valentine's but along with his love and affection that was all I needed this day. I spend the rest of the evening calling my classmate Chelle who recently had her baby to see how she and her baby girl were doing, along with updating her on what's been going on at school.

Also today, Banji our faithful black spaniel had 6 beautiful puppies all boys in the wash room. My sister and I help with the delivery and Mom cleaned the puppies and made sure Banji was comfortable. We have plans to give 4 of them away and keep 2, right now she has to stay inside because it's cold out there.

Feb 15, 1989 Wednesday
Dear Diary,

Today was a day I'll never forget for me. It started out very good at school. Carol, Stephanie and I hung out tripping on everybody during lunch and just making it through the first couple of classes with no problems, I saw Ronnie Brown, and boy was he cute! The problem I was having with him was getting the nerves up to talk; I'm shy as hell when it comes to a guys. I know you're asking why is she talking to another guy and have a boyfriend? Let me see, um Robert was at another school plus I'm not that clueless to think he was faithful, PLEASE! Plus, it's OKAY to have options. Anyway, when I got home at 5:15 p.m. Robert called and said he was coming over. I went crazy trying to fix myself up and looked my best. I can't believe it he's actually coming over!

Around 6:30 p.m., Robert's brother brought him over, at first I was a little surprise, but when this red trick out truck parked in our drive way I was like OMG it's him, this was my first time really seeing Robert since the game and I was completely surprise when I found out how cute he was with beautiful hazel eyes. Anyway, I thought his brother was good-looking. He favored Ralph from New Edition (OKAY I over exaggerated a little on that) now I see why Chelle wanted to get with him so bad. I only wanted to just talk with him, we couldn't go into the bedroom because my sister kept bothering us and we couldn't go in the living room because Cameron was in there, so we stayed in the washroom. We talked in the wash room near the back door; and my sister was being a pest kept bothering me so I told her to stay in her room until my guests leave please. "I know you're thinking, "where is her Mom" this is what happens when a parent work the evening or night shift the kids run wild", back to my story well Robert and I started talking and suddenly he pulled me close and said, "put your lips here and I did with no hesitation then we kissed, WOW.

Honestly that was my first true kiss from a boy. Anyway I wanted to talk but he had something else on his mind instead. He just kept staring at me saying how pretty I was. I never really thought of myself like that just avenge, so it was nice to hear someone say it, anyway he grabs my arm and pulled me closer and ask me to kiss him again, I did and it lasted for almost a minute. We chatted for a while and he started staring at me and then he kisses me over and over again Diane my sister kept calling me for some reason and I told her I'll be there.

A few moments later Robert grab my arm pull me closer I closed the shutters behind us and we kissed more like French kiss for a long time "this was my first French kiss and I'm 16, I don't think it was done right to be honest, but I enjoyed every bit of it". After a couple of kisses and conversation he had to go for (1) my

21

Dear Diary

Mom wasn't home, (2) grandma was probably looking out the kitchen window at the vehicle and (3) I was on cloud nine so none of the other two mattered, I did get my teddy bear after all so today was a good day after all.

Feb 17, 1989 Friday
Dear Diary,

Well today I had a great day thinking about Robert and how special his visit was to me, I really believe we can be happy together he makes me feel like I'm the only thing to him, the thing is I let my insecurity get to me. I want someone to make him feel good, I like when Robert tells me I'm special that is something I don't hear it often enough.

Last night, while on the phone with Robert, he mentioned about having a wet dream about me, I found this very exciting knowing he was having desired feelings for me that left a smile on my face for the rest of the evening. I know it sound weird having someone cream themselves over you, but we are both teenagers with raging hormones all over the place, they have to be release somewhere. Oh yeah school was whatever nothing in particular happen that required my attention to place in the diary today.

Feb 18, 1989 Saturday
Dear Diary,

Well today I had a good day. I woke up around 11 that morning and caught up with the hours and so I looked at a little Soul train, Teen Wolf "this is an animated show starring Michael J. Fox back in the late 80's early 90's you have to be there to enjoy it", so I begin cleaning the kitchen, bathroom and everything else mainly get my chores out of the way before Mom wake up.

I wanted so badly to talk with Robert that I risked going on grandma and leaving my sister whom had the flu at the time by herself just to have a conversation with Robert "now that's puppy love at its finest".

In order for this to work I had to be nice and ask my grandma if she needed anything done, she mentioned to place wood on her back pouch and near the fireplace, to make it easier for her to take wood inside her house. To me that was easy work all I had to do was pulled the wagon over to the wood pile away from the house and load a few pieces on and place them on her pouch, and the next load went in her house in the back room near the fireplace, so after that I ask her "can I use her phone", she said yes, so I called Diane to make sure mama was asleep so anyway,

Authors Note: *"now let me stop here and explain something "why did I go next door to use the phone, let me see my big-headed sister told mama on me about Robert coming over and she grounded me off the phone for 2-weeks"*

I called Robert and he mentioned he just got home at 12:18 p.m. and wanted to finish telling me about the wet dream he had the other night about me, and from what I was hearing it was all that and a bag of chips. He said *"I came over your house and you were the only one home and we walked to the bedroom and I slowly undressed you and became hard instantly after looking at you so I got undress and laid you down on the bed and I got on top of you and we got busy"*, Sounds corny huh, you have to be in my shoes and understand how something like that would turn any girl on. Robert was about to tell me something else, but it couldn't come out, because mama walk in and started bopping me on my head I drop the phone and tried to reach the receiver, but I couldn't reach it so finally I ran out the house and mama was right after me, when we got home she got the switch and hit me a few times and started fussing and cussing about leaving Diane by herself, "like really she was by herself now" I went in the room crying "why did she have to ruin my special Moment" how was I going to explain to Robert why I had to hang up in the middle of our conversation.

I swear dating was difficult back then, no cell phones or computers UGHHH thank god for guys that were thinking ahead. Later after picking up my face I mean pride, I cooked and checked on Diane again before going over to my grandma, she came out and saw me and she busted out laughing at me *"talking about you thought you got away with something didn't you"* while mama was tripping on me she took my phone from me for a few more days DAMN.

Feb 20, 1989 Monday
Dear Diary,

Well today school was OKAY I left my keys at home, which means I had to hang out at my grandmas until Mom came home or just ask grandma for the spare key.

Once I was home it gave me a moment to spend a little time with Banji and her puppies, after I couldn't find anything at home to eat I took my happy self behind back to grandmas' where she had cooked some pork chops w/ gravy on the side rice, butter beans and her golden brown corn bread OMG, after stuffing myself I decided to give Robert a call. We talk from 5:15 till 6 our conversation wasn't much about nothing just wanted to hear his voice.

I mentioned to Robert after realizing how late is was, to call me at home and come to find out the phone was fix it is clear as a bell after not working Sunday; due to a severe thunderstorm. We talked about how he would quit me if I didn't act right, yeah right, not sure what the hell that conversation was about, I didn't have too many explanations to why I was so into Robert, no more than he was cute as hell. My day ended without incident, which is a plus for me especially dealing with a crazy ass mama and a little sister that can't stay in her place sometimes.

Feb 21, 1989 Tuesday
Dear Diary,

Today at school was long and dull; it rained all day I'm not a fan of rainy days unless it's at home. Robert called or rather I called him and we talked until the subject came up about this girl name Candice Jacobs, "Candice is a girl he dated before me and I always felt intimidated by her cause she was an easy fuck. Candice was pretty and older than me" I always kept wondering why he thinking about her and talking to me about it WTH.

I really do care about Robert, but it hurts me to know how she is teasing and carry on with him. I got very upset during our conversation because he couldn't understand why I was feeling so insecure, if he only knew I am a virgin and never been with a boy in any form other than flirting, only to find out his ex is more experience then you and willing to give it up, and to make matters even worse I went to his brother for advise WOW and he is an extreme player, you know I was desperate. At this point in my life I had reasons to feel this way, it was peer pressure to the nine. If you didn't explore it or even attempt to, something is wrong with you, I can't tell you how many times I felt like a LOSER for not going all the way but I was scared plain and simple and I thought you should at least have feeling for the guy before giving it up RIGHT.

Dear Diary

Feb 27, 1989 Monday
Dear Diary,

Today was okay until late that afternoon, I was so sick, with low fever, chills and a cough darn, maybe I caught the flu from Diane I don't know, but I wasn't up to anything just making it through the day and maybe go to school by Wednesday if possible. I manage to feed and care for Banji and her puppies for a while and then around 10:15 p.m. I let her out to do her thing and come back, but around 10:30 p.m. I noticed she went in the woods and got into a fight with another dog (I think); mama, Diane and I stood outside for 30 minutes calling her and there was no reply, since it was dark we couldn't do anything, but wait until the next day and proceed to looked for her. I took a warm bath took some medicine and bed I went.

Feb 28, 1989 Tuesday
Dear Diary,

I woke up feeling worse than yesterday, so I decided to stay home and just rest, besides Mom had already left for work. After getting some orange juice and a toast I went outside to look for Banji. I walked to the edge of the property to hear for her, only to get back silence, the biggest fear is that she's dead somewhere in the woods. God I loved Banji I never thought we would lose her not only that but we will need to care for her 2 little puppies, which are still very young. So I contacted the local Veterinarian to help guide us and provide ways to care for them. We ended up buying baby doll bottles and used a certain type of milk to give them every few hours like a human baby, this was going to be challenging raising them, but they all we have left of Banji.

Lately I have been getting into so much trouble with Mom so much that every little thing in the house that goes wrong she has a fit and get on me like it's always my fault or something that shit is getting old with me, now I was the one sick and she still coming home bitching about the house and etc.,

I kind of think she cares more for my sister then she does for me in a way her attitude is extremely bitter with hatred of some type, I know my sperm donor of a father was an ass-hole, but why put it off on me that's why I get an attitude as well, it hurts a lot I feel like I can't talk to her about anything so mentioning about Robert coming over was out and I didn't bother, "oh what a day". After hearing she was going to be off tomorrow I decided to get better by doping up on medicine, so I can go to school the next day and away from her.

March 1, 1989 Wednesday
Dear Diary,

This morning I woke up feeling totally refresh but still a little drowsy from the meds, but refresh. Today at school was crazy; first off I passed a history test that I barely studied for with an 84% which is good for me. After that, the rest of the day I was able to get with my crew catch up on the latest gossip and trip out on everyone and just have fun.

Robert called, we talked and had an enjoyable conversation that ran over my curfew time (on the phone) but it was a fun conversation, I got too see the crazy side of him and yes those weird feeling come flooding back like I'm going to lose him one day.

One of the things I needed to get past is my damn insecurity issues, it's driving me insane with guilt and god knows it's up to me with controlling myself and not get stupid. Again everything is back to normal, in Terri's world for now.

Dear Diary

March 5, 1989 Sunday
Dear Diary,

Today was okay. I attended church with my sister, the church van came on time and we did our usual Sunday school pickup which included the Clark boys. There were 4 of them and only 3 made me itch, I'm glad they didn't try anything with me, because I wasn't in the mood, I just wanted to get my praise on and go home.

Robert called and we talked a good time but in the middle of our conversation, he requested to talk with mom about coming over to our house for a visit with me. I couldn't believe she said yes, because in her mind "I wanted to meet his little ass and figure out his intentions or whatever", but my mind was on something totally different, I was thinking what would it be feel like to have sex with Robert I mean to feel his arms against my warm body. I wanted to kiss every part of his body and make him get rock hard, I really wanted to feel him and his body on top of me and insert his manhood inside and just move up and down while I just moan in ecstasy over and over again, I wanted him to kiss me where I need it the most have him to satisfy and love me just like that.

Will this fantasy come true or is it just that a fantasy? While all of this is taking place in my mind, mom is still on the phone with Robert, wow you can imagine how I was feeling. Robert and I continue our talk but it only about him coming over my house on when and what time. The excitement of seeing him was clouding my judgment over what I needed to do. I was on cloud nine for the rest of the day, my mom and sister couldn't take my joy, even if they tried.

March 6, 1989 Monday
Dear Diary,

Today was okay sometimes I dislike my cousin Tricia's because of her behavior today, she is such a slut for as long as I've known her. I found out she was sleeping with this new guy that transferred from Miami to our school in Georgia this semester.

Keith was a cutie and a lot of girls were fascinated with the fact he's from Miami, now rumors were going around the baby she's carrying was his WOW. I honestly didn't know they knew each other like that or even manage to sleep together.

Keith didn't want to claim his baby by Tricia and the bad part about it is if the baby is his he is going to leave and go back to Miami, because he thinks she was messing around and what they had was a one-night stand between them, she was with him even with all the times he talked about how nasty the girls he messed with looked now, look at her WOW. That was a history lesson for later; the important thing was getting the nerve to write David a letter just to expressing my interest in him. David is a guy whom I played with when I was much younger.

I was a Tomboy at heart until I turned 12 and David was the guy I begin to look different at. It was a weird feeling for me, it was the day I changed into a girl. It was the summer of 1988, the guys asked me to come out and play soft ball with them; "because they know I have a mean arm of course". I put on my shortest shorts and fix my hair up for the first time to look like a young lady, instead of playing games with the guys, like I usually do I opt to just stare and clap for David and he found that extremely odd and began questioning me on "why are you dress like that, and I thought you were playing, what gives", OMG that was embarrassing, even for me to explain why, he came over to the house we talked and stuff, but later on he's just a friend and I wanted to keep it that way, besides my feelings for Robert are so different they are deeper, after understanding what was going on with me I decided to put all my attention to Robert and put away crazy thoughts of others.

Dear Diary

March 7, 1989 Tuesday
Dear Diary,

School was okay this guy name Breeze whose sort of popular at the school talked to me for the first time. He was a brother that could talk a girl out of her underwear, if you let him. I thought it was cute and I played the game right along with him. I saw Ron again and it made that weird feeling come over me but nothing to turn my feelings away from Robert that was only getting stronger. I'm not sure why I had to say this, as if to remind myself that I had a boyfriend" Robert told me he feels the same way and I don't want to lose him. Unlike school my home life was still difficult to understand; I was just going through the motions hoping it would get better. I didn't get a chance to chat with Robert cause of how late it was, so I just grab my teddy bear and went off to sleep, thinking of the next day.

March 9, 1989 Thursday
Dear Diary,

Today was crazy at school; hell it was beginning to look crazy to me. First, Keith was giving off this weird vibe like he was feeling me or something, I didn't have the slightest idea why, I just saw him as a good friend and that's it. Ron, my goodness I got to stay away from him he's such a snobbish guy I've ever meant that's why I can't put my energy into him, on to more important business.

Last night, I talked to Robert in a cruel and harsh way, I care about the "Kid" but what I hear about his brother sometimes I think he's in that category a straight player, so I don't trust him and was not trying to give him the chance too. I think of what transpired during the day got to me and I was a little emotional and plus it was that time of the month.

Dear Diary

March 10, 1989 Friday
Dear Diary,

Today was a good day especially after I look at Derrick "Dirk" Jones. He's still cute in more ways than one, he lost a lot of weight and his hair is shaved off because he enlisted in the Army. Before I go further, let me give a brief tale on Mr. Jones, he was the guy I was flirting with heavily.

Derrick was a senior and the jock of the school and me a little ole freshman, I had a thing for older guys, because I felt my peers didn't know any better. We flirted a few times in between classes and I make eye contact with him a couple of times, but nothing more. Derrick was the first guy I let explore my pleasure spot and almost gave up the goodies for.

Before Robert and I got together, one night during a school Dance. I ran into him and I ran over and spoke. Derrick kept looking me up and down, so he suggested we go somewhere private, *"sure let's go"* I said. Dirk took me to his car that was parked behind the school, he opened the door and allowed me in and I was totally nervous, like OMG this going to totally happen (losing my virginity of course), he climbed in and turned on the radio and begins staring at me. I started talking and his lips touched mine I was so nervous; I didn't know what to do but let my body take control. We were fine just kissing, he begin lifting my dress up and touching me but then Dirk pulled a move that disturb the whole grove to where I was feeling a little uncomfortable, Dirk unzip his pants and pull his penis out to put the rubber on and stop anything from happening further OMG I freaked the hell out and pulled my dress down and bounce, one I was a virgin only saw a penis in the nasty books never live, and when I saw his it was huge and I freaked; my bad it was too much too soon, and I left him right there in the car with his pants down and privates up.

31

Dear Diary

Of course complications ensured, my cousin Tony saw me leaving the car and assumed something happened. The next day word got around the school and I was horrified, but then Dirk didn't deny it which made me sort of popular my conscience at that moment wouldn't allow me to tell the truth, due to the fact I wanted to feel included I accepted the rumor. When me and my friends were in the court yard I could feel him looking at me, even though it will be hard to get Derrick off my body it's easy to get him off the brain once I learned about his girlfriend, yeah he had one of those. To make a long story short, I changed my actions and begin focusing more on my studies. I was entering the 10 grade and SAT wasn't far so getting my grades up was important.

March 14, 1989 Tuesday
Dear Diary,

Well today was okay school being fair as usual I got my report card today and in all my classes nice grades, 1st period a 93, 2nd period 88, 3rd period 78, 4th period 89, 5th period 91 and in 6th period a 73, my last period messed me up I passed all his tests except one and on home work assignments, oh well at least Mom would be happy to see no F's.

Robert had a problem first he calls me with an attitude talking about I'm going to bust you up I guess that was his way of joking with me whatever and later in the day he called to tell me he's going to Tallahassee and going to stay half the night there. OKAY now at this point I wanted to tell him I missed and want him next to me, I feel desperate sometimes, but why should I he has this and that girl why should I be upset that's why when he goes somewhere I know it's to be with another girl, I suck at this.

32

Dear Diary

March 16, 1989 Thursday
Dear Diary,

Today was good I taking a math test and passed, yes because I studied hard for it. The rest of day of smooth sailing all I wanted to do was go home and relax a moment and hear from Robert, he called this morning at 6:25 a.m. I was shock we talked for 5 min. and I really like Robert but I want to see him more and more. I told Robert he was hurting me and I couldn't stand the thought of not seeing him.

If only he knew how I felt so alone without him beside me. I wanted him as my friend, lover, and boyfriend. When I'm at school I go into space wondering how I can get to him, it hurts sometimes just to hear his voice and imaging his smile. I told Robert how deeply I cared about him but I knew that our relationship was different in so many ways. I love Robert for being patient with me, because sometimes at night I keep wondering how it would feel to be with him one whole day without anyone but me and him, just me and Robert.

March 18, 1989 Saturday
Dear Diary,

Well today was somewhat normal and boring at the same time, living out in the country is a retired person's dream, but a teenagers' nightmare, there was nothing out here to do fun at my age but stay coupe up in the house was what it was.

I called Robert and told him that I was coming over his house after I asked my mom if it was OK if she stop by there, she said yes, but a yes usually end up to be whatever, and of course I didn't show because we went to one of my Mom's friends Mrs. Elisa but she wasn't home we went to Quincy to buy Alexander O'Neal album and it's good so I pass Robert's house coming back and Cameron was in the car I guess just chilling and his sister were out the front playing. I ask Mom to drop me off and she said that I was too young and shouldn't be going to see guys true, but Robert don't have a way, so we just went home instead.

Can you believe the switch and swap she pulled, I was frustrated with mom that after returning home, I called Robert and told him what happened he seem to understand, but it still bothered me?

March 19, 1989 Sunday
Dear Diary,

Well today was an average day, church was nice and good and so I listen to a little of Alexander O'Neal until grandma got a little tired, I wasn't allowed to listen to mom record player because she was asleep from night shift work. Instead I ran in and called Robert he was a little upset cause I didn't come over, I tried to explain but I don't think it worked mama had an attitude but whatever I call Robert again, and we talked until he told me about the phone call from a girl name Vivian, like I suppose to care, I don't mind having someone that girl's go crazy for, but it doesn't matter if he told me or not. I really do care about him I know every time I write in this book it's the same old thing, but I love to express my feelings for this guy.

Tonya came today and we went to Havana and we wanted to see some guys so we went downtown into Harvey's because that's where they hang out so we meet these guys name Travis & Michael, we had fun talking to them and I got home and call Mark to play with, I don't think he likes Tonya the way she handles him oh well mama wanted me to help clean the house we did and it looked beautiful, mama also found my ring that I lost so I pretend I didn't know it was missing, she brought for me for my birthday and I lost it maybe two weeks later.

Later Diane came and we sat in the room and watch TV with me and we chilled until around 9:00 p.m. so I called Robert, but he couldn't talk until about 9:45 apparently his brother was hogging the phone until around 11:00 p.m. and then Robert return my call. I was able to get some of what I wanted to say until mama wanted to use the phone, so Robert said *"I love you"*, and I replied the same with the phone tone going blank. I hope tomorrow is better.

March 20, 1989 Monday
Dear Diary,

Well school was okay and life is beautiful to me it is. I got a good nap in 5th Period and cheated big time on a history test bad Terri, whatever a girl got a do what a girl got to do. Tonya was having a problem with what she wanted to do when Henry gets home; he's her boyfriend coming home for a weekend spell from the military.

Things were making no sense at all with Robert, for instance, I called to see if he was home and he wasn't so I called Tonya and talked with her for a few moments about Henry and other things, she had to run an errand and called it an evening. Robert, still didn't call so I figure I should. When I found out he was home I got a little attitude, I mean he could have called, so I said *"I have to eat and I'll talk with you later"*.

He is kind of doing the same thing he did with Vera treated her in way to get off the line just to talk to me, but if he is talking to another girl should I worry. I told him about his negative attitude and he claim he loves me, there's not much love in the world, but I figure he say it as words that are true just to keep me near. I'm beginning to understand this relationship thing, one it's complicated as hell and very time consuming too much for a young to take.

Dear Diary

March 22, 1989 Wednesday
Dear Diary,

Today was an ok day; school was nice I'm taking my BHS test over writing. I hope this time my score is better.

OMG Robert is a low down son of a bitch; he has been putting me on hold for the last three days. I'm not sure yet if he's communicating with Ms. Thang again at first I didn't care if Robert was talking to someone, but now it's messing with my personal time. Anyway, my suspension for Robert not calling me has to do with someone else, but I'm not sure yet; Robert is making it difficult and have the nerve to expect me to feel good about it too.

Finally, the little bastard called to talk around 11:38 pm, hell I'm in the bed trying to get my rest for school the next day or you kidding me. My first question to his little ass was seeing or talking to another girl and needed his damn space; he exclaims *"no I was just busy with track and singing with my cousins in Quincy"*, I told him how hurt I was over it, so I made him apologize even fake crying a little to make the scene better. He was telling me how much he loves me and even sang the song they were working on, I was still mad but satisfied over the results, we stayed on the phone till 1 a.m. and I was able to get up Thurs. morning for school.

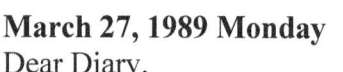

March 27, 1989 Monday
Dear Diary,

Today was a very hard day for me. School seems to never end and the testing my goodness it was taking forever to complete. I spend 3 periods in the testing area trying finish up. I may have failed Math, cause of my erasers mark and plus it neither's my strong subject nor is English; *"lord please let me pass, AMEN"*. After all the testing from this morning I took a must needed nap in 6th period and felt refresh just in time to go home.

Dear Diary

I got home to check out everything mom bought and see what was cooking; she had some nice flowers arranged in the living room to give that ambiance. Robert called at 5:25pm I couldn't talk, I had shit to do, plus it was more of getting back at him for not calling me, so after completing my chores and homework I decided to call him around 9:00 p.m. on for him to tell me he was going to stay over in Quincy till Friday so he could compete in an out of town Track-meet, I said *"that's cool I have something to keep me occupied"*, yeah right, honestly I was feeling all alone, he's gone but what else can I do but stay focus.

March 30, 1989 Thursday
Dear Diary,

Well today at school was good, this guy name Chris is super cute, but I never thought Lorenzo like me and I was going to be a fool and tell him to fix me up with Chris. Today on the bus Ree told me "he likes me" and I said "Oh really" but I want to talk to Chris not Lorenzo damn, it's driving me crazy to figure this out he and get caught, plus Barbara will see him with me and tell Robert and I'm not ready to break up with him yet.

I tried with him before and it didn't work and now whatever. Chris looked so adorable and I hope him and Angela have split up, because he is so cute and fine smart too. I had a nice day and this is the third day and I miss Robert, I hope he misses me like I do. Now I see why Robert always want me over to his house because mostly all his girlfriends have and I'm not going so I will stay in my place.

March 31, 1989 Friday
Dear Diary,

Today was nice; testing was finally over for me I can relax YESSSS. I miss Robert so much wishing he wasn't in Quincy, but beside me. Friday is the Shin-dig in Bainbridge and I wanted to see Robert there, I want him to take me home and take me there, so we can at least know more about each other. I went with my cousin instead and enjoyed the festivities.

Lufo and his frat group step it was nice, everyone was there mainly my friend from school. After coming home, I was reminded about Robert and how I couldn't stand the thought of not seeing him hoping his brother could pick me up and drop him off my house so we can talk about the things we have been missing out on maybe kiss a little neck a little something like that, hoping he can cure what's been stirring up inside us. I told him I loved him dearly and I wanted to show him how much I do, oh well my wishing may come true one day.

April 1, 1989 Saturday
Dear Diary,

Well today was a crazy day first I was scared to call Robert and everything due to I haven't talked to him in a couple of days. Instead I called Tonya and she told Lorenzo to find out some information on Chris.

Chris is this guy at school who I found extremely cute, I've been eyeing him for some time now and wanted to know more about him. Well anyway she called and told me everything, what he said was Chris wasn't feeling me that way and just wanted to be friends; FINE.

Instead of being piss about him, I decided to call Robert, big mistake he didn't have anything to say so I hung up on him too, damn this is not turning out good today. His brother Cameron is putting stuff in his head as if he's the man and I should bow down to Robert, please. I realize I have options here, Chris is a cutie and I'm able to see him every day, Robert has my heart and I shouldn't be pushing up on Chris so fast, because something nasty might come out of this that I'm not ready for.

Dear Diary

April 2, 1989 Sunday
Dear Diary,

Today was a chilling day; Robert wanted to know what was up with me for not calling him back and being short with him on the phone. I told him I loved him and all was good just things weren't making sense. I was letting my suspensions cloud my judgment and think the worse of Robert instead of just owning it.

I feel like if I'm not able to give Robert sex like he wants we won't be a couple anymore. Robert explains to me that am not the case and he loving the relationship we have because it's innocent and not rushed. I felt at ease with his words, but that evil insecure side is still tapping me on the shoulders telling me otherwise damn her.

Lorenzo my freshman classmate is falling hard for my cuz talking about for her sexy voice and all, I thought he was funny as hell and had no chance with her. Lorenzo told me he'll corporate with me on setting things up with Chris, he's such a cutie. I want Lorenzo to only tell him things about me and not show him to me until I see fit frankly if he did see it would probably start a stir sense he is a freshman. I wouldn't mind to just have him as my friend instead of my boyfriend, if he wants Lorenzo first to get some information like phone number and girlfriend birthday something I'll get a name.

Well that my day even though I was supposed to have gone skating, but I didn't want to go until Wed. Later on Robert called and he had an attitude about the way our situation was taking place, but forgets that mess, if Lorenzo play his cards right things will go good for me and Chris hopefully and Robert well.

Dear Diary

April 5, 1989 Wednesday
Dear Diary,

Today was suppose of been the day we go to the skating ring because I got into trouble with mom for going into her locked room yesterday took some mouth wash and I forgot to lock it back. I'm not sure why she locked it anyway seriously, honestly mom had nicer things in her room then our bathroom, so it was obvious I was going to go in, I just didn't expect all this to happen with her being real mad, it's like the older I get the more the angrier she is. I wanted to leave since I was thirteen, but I could never go because I didn't have enough money or faith in people to help.

So now that I'm sixteen collecting money has been even harder I have $10.50 a bus fare is $15.00 or more and I've already written a letter to my grand-dad in Tampa wanting him to come get me. Things are going to get more and more hectic then they already are, she has even taking the phone calling herself teaching me a lesson in which I would get back by Sat., or when in a better mood. I hope Aunt Earline tell Tonya I'm not going to the Skating Ring after all. All this because for mouthwash darn.

April 7, 1989 Friday
Dear Diary,

Today I had a frightening experience with someone that I have been having a torch for since the day I saw him. I'm waiting for him to make his move, but I'm afraid I'm wasting it today Diane my sister had to get her hair done at the local unisex salon in Bainbridge and I had to go with her, while mom continue shopping. I was getting bored the minute I got there, but I kept myself occupied by looking at Young & the Restless on TV. Phillip, a classmate from school tried to cheer me up with conversation and a few nice look guys came in but nothing like Chris.

Dear Diary

I wasn't expecting him to come through and oh my god I almost lost it he got a box like hair cut and was looking extra cute. Mrs. Deloris was finish with Diane's hair so I look up at him dead in his face and of course he was looking, I begin to scream with excitement inside all while this was happening I noticed the other guys checking as well, which I was totally ignoring. All while my sister sat there getting her final touches I kept my eyes down cause if I looked up OMG I wanted to look, but couldn't *(man what is wrong with me)* I couldn't find my voice, I couldn't wait to leave, because he was too cute. I can't wait to tell Tonya and Diane mentioned after we left, he didn't look at me, but he did I know he did. Wow that was a good day.

Chris Johnson
&
Terri Williams

Authors Note: ***"As I mentioned earlier ladies, I was young and clueless meaning I didn't know the difference between flirting and falling for a guy. I was in love before even speaking to the guy and already I'm talking about Chris & Terri WTH"***.

Dear Diary

April 10, 1989 Monday
Dear Diary,

Today was misty and wet there was an over-cast all day and it was Moms birthday is today she's turning 38. School was the usual Lorenzo was watching following my cousin Tonya like he was crazy or something and Chris well I don't know, I'm scared he's going to do me like Cedric did. We did hit it off fine, but I was self conscience and didn't want people wondering; "why is he talking to her of all people" and I don't want that to happen. That was something I needed to work on getting past the bad things and not looking at the good in which I knew was there.

After school, I notice mom's old school music Bobby Womack playing and she was cooking up something it smelled good; Diane and I made a cake which was sort of cute and tasty. After eating dinner mom blowing out the candles we decided to remind her how old she was getting, that didn't go to well but she was still happy; in fact, so happy she decided to top the evening off by taking her bottle of wine and going into the room, why anything to keep from doing nothing I'm with it, oh yea I got my phone back (what I tell ya). While cleaning the kitchen, Robert called we chatted for a moment, until he made me mad instead of getting piss with him I just told him hey mom's birthday today so let's continue this piss fest later. So today was a good day!

April 11, 1989 Tuesday
Dear Diary,

Today wasn't so bad even though Lorenzo forgot about me and Chris. I saw him between classes but I dared not to speak. He looks so quiet and cute till the point I start to question that maybe he's too good for me, he's smart, mature and he hang with this snobbish group, his last girlfriend was a very smart and pretty girl and all but I'm trying to see where I could fit in. One thing's for sure I needed to work on getting my friendship back on track with Carol we had a disagreement late last week and hadn't talked since, after sitting with during lunch by 5th Period everything was cool again. Robert called but we couldn't talk very long had to do a chore first.

April 17, 1989 Monday
Dear Diary,

Today was good. To begin Lorenzo gave my number to Chris and during 5th Period he was hanging out with some guys; I was so nervous to face him that I started speed walking through the hall not knowing he was right behind me and stuff and as I was going in the building he scraps his finger against me all while giving me a look and walk off, OMG I almost freaked out like what just happen. After school when I got on the bus Lorenzo said Chris said he was going to call me. I thought to myself this can't be happening right, but then my whole face was flushed red from embarrassment, I was just smiling the whole ride home.

I started handling all my chores and my homework anticipating a call, but sitting there waiting for the phone to ring was beginning to bore me a little. Finally, after 6:15 pm he called, Chris "Is this Terri", Terri "yes this is her", Chris "hi girl what's up", at this point I'm like ok Chris was nothing like what I expect him to be innocent type with the straight face, but goodness this guy got a mouth on him, I mean he was cussing and carry on like we have been talking forever. Chris was stunned that I had a crush on him and thought it different to have a girl give her number. I was smiling from ear to ear the entire conversation because I was nervous for no reason.

This is what happens when I allowed my mind to take control over. I'm happy me and Chris finally talked it gave me peace of mind that he wasn't a jerk, so overall the phone call was the best.

Oh about Robert I didn't talk to him and even if I did it wouldn't of matter, I was still on cloud nine from Chris.

April 18, 1989 Tuesday

Dear Diary,

Well today was very great day. I see Chris he asks me to wait for him at the window after class, I asked my cousin to wait with me because I was still nervous and didn't want to look like a fool waiting by myself. After awhile I was getting tired and I to make the next class before the bell ring, while I preparing to leave he came up and grab me and pull me back, talking about *"I told you to wait"*, really um class starts in 2 min. so any way we chanted for a while and I left to get into the classroom.

After 5th period I stood waiting for him and we walked to our next class, after 5th period I was walking out the door and Chris came up behind me and told me to stop for a minute so we walked toward the door, Chris said "call me tonight", with my cool self I said "alright sure", even though I was screaming inside over it like really he wanted me to call him, LOL. Once I was done with my homework, I called Robert his mom answered the phone and told me Robert's on punishment and can't get on the phone, aww poor baby, oh well I'm good. I called Chris and guess what, he was looking for my phone call I was surprised and God him and Robert are so much alike but anyway I was joking around with him about something and finally he said "when are you going to get serious" I said "I am serious with you, but are you with me", we have to learn each other before anything serious come to hand and I hope you don't like going fast. I think he likes me if not he wouldn't be calling me or walking me to class. OMG he is so cute…

Dear Diary

April 19, 1989 Wednesday
Dear Diary,

Today at school was cool well anyway I didn't see Chris until 2nd Period he didn't notice me one part of me feels good about talking to him and the other part makes me feel like I'm a joke because I think he know I'm not stupid, when I'm around him I get very nervous for no reason at all so at 5th Period as I was walking to class he seems not interested in talking to me, but he manages so I thought I shouldn't call, but I think I should, it's getting late so I didn't. I decided to call and he claim he was waiting for me and that I was tripping OKAY NOT, while we were talking I call him Keith instead of Chris and he was tripping we had a good conversation after that and it was all good.

Authors Note: *"Now during this entry, my deep insecurities were starting to show. Chris didn't even notice me until later, but in my mind I was seeing it differently. This is why you should have confidence in yourself before entering into any relationship, it's one of the reasons why I was thinking and doing things that didn't make sense".*

Dear Diary

April 22, 1989 Saturday
Dear Diary,

I had a very interesting day, I went to get my hair done at Michelle's she seems nice I got a wash n curl which came out pretty, I was totally impress with the results I wanted to show them off, too bad it was Sat. and waiting for Monday will not keep this hairstyle. I found out Deloris is pregnant again for the same guy because he got another girl pregnant and her last baby isn't a year-old wow man and all this and she's in the 10th grade crazy.

I didn't call Chris because I felt bad about Friday and didn't want to further embarrass myself so good for me. Tasha invited me to her slammer party at her house, it was okay all my friends were there Lank, Debra, Sharon, Muddy; we watched a few movies, ate pizza and begin messing with the drinks by putting salt and ketchup in them I was wondering why it tasted so awful. We watched "Golden Child", "School Daze and "First Blood" after that we started to go back to bed around 3:15 am but so as soon we got back in the room we begin talking about sex, boyfriends and singing so at 4:00 a.m. we cut out the lights and start tripping on each other boyfriends, they started primping up Debra hair it was a trip so while we're doing all of that we were still tripping so until 5:30 am I finally fell asleep and we woke up at 11:30 am, it was cool we ate breakfast and went our separate ways.

That was a nice sleepover, because it gave us a chance to know each other better. I came home and called Robert just to catch up on what's been going on with him, we talked a lot and I was able to reconnect with him. I still have my baby Robert which was nice. Chris, yeah I'm going to leave that alone for awhile just to see what's up with Robert first.

April 24, 1989 Monday
Dear Diary,

Today was very nice for me I was happy all day. For one, Chris approached me after 1st Period he didn't say anything just smiling his ass off, which left me dam confused, so after 3rd Period we walked around the building to my next class and Chris was in a good mood, we kind of caught up from last week which was nice.

Well after 6th Period and when I got on the bus Lorenzo handed me a note from Chris where it wasn't much so at 6:00 pm, he called and was tripping with me and I was too, it was a good conversation but anyway he said *"I like you because of your humor"*, I was totally blushing inside over that, "he liked me really" well after that I felt good. I had to end the call early because my cousin Ken came over our house with his girlfriend Toni. She was a very pretty girl, they both attended FAMU and he wanted to introduce her to grandma and mama (which mean this girl is the real for him to bring her here) and of course I got some money. I didn't call Robert it was late and I was tired maybe tomorrow.

April 26, 1989 Tuesday
Dear Diary,

Well today was shitty, Chris got upset at me about something unpredictable and well he dodges me all day I've had this done to me before, but this time fuck it if he feels that way about it fine. Tomorrow I'm not going to be the nice person to nobody; Chris bet not let me see his ass.

Dear Diary

Authors note: *My mind was playing tricks on me again and it was only going to get worse.*

May 1, 1989 Monday
Dear Diary,

Well today was okay, Chris well I got things back on track for now, with it raining like crazy today my hair fell and well I made an A+ on my Math test and tonight I called Chris we had a nice talk. I hope things work out.

May 4, 1989 Thursday
Dear Diary,

Well today was nice and well Chris ya well he's was bugging again, he noticed me at the snack machine and he was so close to me I thought we were going to kiss, but I wasn't that tempting so after class he pass by me he later said "you could have stood there" seeing how long he was going to walk and well he was smiling so I figure he knew I was back. Robert was able to get back on the phone again and things were bad between me and Chris. Can't the world just end now?

Dear Diary

May 5, 1989 Friday
Dear Diary,

Well today was cool a little, Chris has such a nice way of dumping a girl, he didn't say a word to me also he didn't even look at me today. I felt bad but I shouldn't I mean he's not what I thought he would be instead he's just like the other guys that I know. At one point I was beginning to think Chris thought I was a loose girl and maybe wanted some ass, but since I was playing hard to get or whatever he decided to move on, shit and here I was wondering if I wasn't cute enough for his ass.

I was acting stupid around him why I don't know just childish I guess. I mean he treated me so nice for two days out of a week and the rest fuck you, he treats me like nothing happened. I liked him not because he was cute yes it is, but he makes me laugh and at other times I want to kill him if I call him how would he react, would he be the same or perk up a to my voice or what.

Okay this is what I'll do disguise my voice and be Tonya or I might just tell him it's me to see how he would feel, how to start the conversation off is another one I haven't gotten yet okay let me try this:

"Hello Chris you might not know me, but this is Tonya", "so how are you doing tonight so Chris how are things going with you and Terri, Chris I know you are thinking about her."

What the hell am I doing making up imaginary conversations to make a boy talked to me, dam I need help. I've come to a conclusion that me and Chris were just made up, I knew he was way out of my league but I wanted to try anyway his friends thought of me as something else, but I had to know for myself.

Dear Diary

May 8, 1989 Monday
Dear Diary,

Today was a great day for me, first of all Chris wasn't on my mind till after 2nd Period. In Science class we free time and we started tripping on everybody Mr. Frazier is a trip, he let us have our fun. School ended up being nice, my hair stayed neat and fresh all day but I knew one thing I'm not going to let a boy like Chris ruin it steals my joke believe that.

May 12, 1989 Friday
Dear Diary,

Today was okay, I didn't see Chris and wasn't really caring, but anyway when I got home we went to Bainbridge and had fun and stuff with my cousin so later on that night mama ask me why haven't the phone been ringing off the hook with Chris and Robert calling so to keep her out of my business I call Robert, it wasn't like I wanted to talk to him so I told him "I'll talk with you later on", he called around 1:00 a.m. I had to catch the phone on the first ring and the fact it was late I'm surprise I was up still.

Robert and I had a lovely conversation, he was talking so soft and I was falling asleep from it, but then all of a sudden the phone call changed and he was making me weird inside like whoa I'm feeling sort of good here maybe it's song that is on "Can you Stand the rain" by New Edition for some reason I had that sexual type feeling come over and he was telling me how he wanted to hold my hand, hug and kiss me. Robert expressed how we could do things together with each other bodies. Then I told him that, "every time I think or talk about you only one thing comes to mind "SEX" that's all I think about especially having it with you", the conversation got more and more steamy every minute after he woke me up he fell asleep and so I told him I loved him for cheering me up, I don't but somehow I have this intense desire to

50

be with him and I want more with him. After 10 months of going with him and not being with him is causing me to go into a sexual peak for him, I'm a virgin and I want to give myself to him.

Sometimes I feel real love for him and then I don't besides not see him make it worse. I want Robert to have me in complete ecstasy; I want him to be close to me and nothing more.

May 14, 1989 Sunday
Dear Diary,

Well as you may know we had a boring time until about 8:30 p.m. we went to Tallahassee and ate at Burger King and so later on that night I called Robert @ 11:50 p.m. thinking he wouldn't be at home instead he was and we talked until about 12:58 p.m. so anyway I had so much fun maybe tomorrow will be better.

May 15, 1989 Monday
Dear Diary,

Well I had fun today, first I passed Reading test, but failed the math test by 3 points. I wasn't studying until about 5th Period he come in smiling like I'm doing something, well I got home to see what happen to mama and her blood just went up and I wasn't in the mood to find out what the problem was so I called Robert and he went to sleep on me. I want him to send something of himself by Margaret tomorrow I'll see how that will go.

May 16, 1989 Tuesday
Dear Diary,

Hi well today at school was nice and everything Chris didn't come good and Vera has her eyes on this man rather than Robert and well Tonya gotten her Senior pictures and they looked very nice too and well Tonya and Theodor are somewhat tying the knot

Dear Diary

and well me I rather stay single then go with these nutty boys just for something I call Robert and well he said he would call me right, but today was nice.

CHAPTER 5

Phone sex
May 18, 1989 Thursday
Dear Diary,

Well last night I had an interesting talk with Robert from 12:00 till 2:38 a.m. I confessed to him that I was a virgin and he seems a little shock hear that, after a moment of silence, Robert said in a smooth tone "I loves virgins, if you get them first they would always come back", I told him "oh really and how you figure that", he said, "because they might be afraid to try someone else", I still didn't understand his rational thoughts about that. While I was laughing over Roberts thoughts, he begins to change the mood by introducing me to place I didn't think existed.

Robert begin the tale of our first encounter and well he was telling me how he wanted to get me in a dark room and kiss me by slowly taking his shirt off and slowly caressing me into his arms and he said he would kiss my breasts and fumble my nibbles until they became on hard and he said as I get on top of you and move my head inside, but not too deep and would ask me does it hurt and then he would go deeper I would say yes so he would and well I lost control of my desires and went into a uncontrollable ecstasy he made me so wet, all while I was losing my mind I notice Robert was actually on hard and started breathing hard and talking low and I couldn't control myself.

Dear Diary

I let my feelings and the moment get the best of me. I'm not even sure this was possible, but the experience was worth it. I felt truly in love with him and it hurts to know that I can't get to him. He also told me that since I was a virgin then he wants to be gentle with me and caring, slow and show how much he loved me. I can say this was my first phone sex experience and gosh it was exciting.

May 20, 1989 Saturday
Dear Diary,

Today was nice my cousins from Orlando were visiting and Donna and I had a nice conversation, basically catching up. I wasn't a fan of my distant relatives, because they were more citified and well me country as hell, it was exhausting being friendly so I took a good nap.

Tonya called and we talk about Keith and boy did we have fun tripping about that, well so it was about 8:30 when they left well later on that night Robert called around 10:30 p.m. we talked up a storm about he couldn't make me hot and I could so he was breathing funny and hard which was making me crazy wanting him we talked till 4:30 and well at that point he was breathing up something sending chills down my spine but we had to end it WOW.

CHAPTER 6

Sharing Each Other
May 21, 1989 Sunday Part I
Dear Diary,

Today was okay and it was one I may not forget. I woke up late around 1:00 p.m.; I totally missed church so I bathe, cook and everything and later found out my cousin Donna left at 11:00 a.m. so I just put all my focus on Robert, who promised he was going to come over today.

It was around 2:30 p.m. when I heard his dad truck pulled up with him in it. I begin to panic, especially with mom there. She got a change to meet Robert and talked with his dad since she knew him from school. I brought Robert into our living room and we sat down, he was dressed casual with this breath taking cologne on that was hypnotizing me, I was so drawn in especially with his eyes, wow they had me for a moment, while I was talking he leaned over and kissed me, I didn't know how to respond so we begin to messing around we chatted for a couple of minutes until he wanted to use the bathroom and well when I got around the corner to see if he was OK, he grabbed me and we kissed again, this time I could feel his penis getting hard every minute. I wanted to just fall, instead we came back in the living room sat down.

Robert, started caressing my cheeks softly and he being roaming his hands over my breasts and waist and well we began French kissing hard and it felt good; all while this was happening he begin running his hands around my shorts and pulling on them saying "this is good for me to stick my hands down there and go for it" WHAT is he suggesting what I think he is yes (finger fuck). Robert proceeds to kiss me and run his hand on me and suddenly I felt his fingers in me and OMG goodness, he was going so deep I could feel it. The sensation sent chills down my spine, Robert repeated this over and over until I begin scratching his back and of course this left weeps on his back, what did he expect not only that he put two passion marks on me.

I hope I can keep this from mama they are my first ones. If mama knew how we were carry on she would've killed both of us. She called me once and asks me what was all that bumping about and why is your hair messed up; I was so embarrassed like really, she said her and Abe didn't carry on like you two are doing. At that point I figured, she knew. So after all that 15 min later his dad came, Robert stayed for 2 hrs and they were the best, man what else good can happen.

Sharing Each Other
May 21, 1989 Sunday Part II.
Dear Diary,

I never really told you the full story of what happen between me and Robert, well to begin he came at 3:18 p.m. and he was dress nice and was so cute to me he is well as I was joining him in the living room I got a book and start reading up something and he was playing around with my nose by poking at it every time I got smart with him and then I started playing with his hair which he did mess up and so well he ask me to kiss him and I did we French kiss for a few seconds and I heard mama so she was in the bathroom when I went to get a cup of tea to wet me throat.

So as I sat down Robert begin playing or may I say started rubbing my legs and pulling my shorts talking about how big they were so I got interested and ask Robert to put a hickey on my neck, so he did it was short, because mama came in the kitchen for something to eat. After she left Robert was talking about how pretty he did the hickey so he wanted to use the bathroom I said "sure it's right there" he wanted me to go with him so I did and got around the corner and he begin to French kiss this time a minute in a half he was pressing my body against his. I could feel his penis grow hard under me and it seem as though he wanted to get me then.

Dear Diary

He came over and sat beside me and we continue to talk and so he was fumbling with my shorts with his hands he said "this is good for me to stick my hands here and you know", I'm like "Okay" we begin to trip again until I ask him to put another one here and god when he did he was teasing at my neck gently biting it, he begin breathing hot on my neck which made me wet instance I wanted that so he lift up I kiss him because it stirred something up inside that was making me wild inside, we kissed a long time and Robert's hand was roaming all over my body I couldn't resist he was rubbing my breasts until they swell with pleasure. He begin sliding down my stomach onto my leg which he put his hand down and begin touching, stroking and rubbing me harder until he plunge his fingers into me I wanted to moan so bad but couldn't in fear of mama hearing me, so instead Robert started kissing me instead to keep me quiet I was grabbing his back scratching him ever y inch he went in deeper he later place my hands on his already bulging penis it was in a good size and so I rub to see how long it was a good length for me anyway so I later on he put his down my pants again and rub me gentle and plunge in so I scratch him he was going in and out of me, so I was rubbing on his penis and I felt he was wet so I stop and so then let out a moan that made him put his finger into me again so anyway I ask Robert why did you do that he said to see how deep I was and couldn't take it like measuring him, after all that excitement he ask me to check out his back and it was pretty messed up WOW, well I know I had the time of my life and he left at 5:09 p.m.

May 28, 1989 Sunday
Dear Dairy,

Hi today seem to be such a nice day well we looked at Coming to America which I liked a lot it was funny after that we looked at Child's Play it was alright not that scary either, on Robert well he is so young, but he is so intelligent bright and he is so mature to be

14 he seems to young well like when he came over here and we did what we did he did it so good I mostly forgot how young he was he makes me feel so good inside and I'm falling deeply in love with him.

I know he going to say he won't hurt me but how do I know that if I express my feeling too much to him he might use it against me I really do love him so much and want to stay with him as long as I can I want him to know how I really feel as if he's my friend my man and my future lover. He acts more mature than any of those losers at school. This is our 11 month together and I want it to be one day soon, well I hope that we would always be together.

Terri Williams

Robert Thomas

May 31, 1989 Tuesday
Dear Dairy,

Well today was nice I had a good time at school tripping with my friends and everything, later in the day I called my baby to see was he busy instead he was looking at Rocky III so around 11:08 p.m. he called me back. I was up and well Robert he wanted to be honest with me and tell me how he felt.

With that if I told you my deepest feelings for you would he hurt me in anyway he said "I would never hurt you Terri", I was touch so I told him how I felt which was all true I do know why I love Robert so much he's kind, gentle, intelligent and easy to talk to and so I told him about a commitment in our relationship and Robert told me he would give me his necklace I would like that. My heart has a deep question for Robert, like is he the guy I should give my virginity to or not I want too.

While Robert and I were talking I got turned on and so was he, he was hot and bothered before I was and get this he was more into

Dear Diary

it, well Robert wanted to hear me say I love you so I did he began to get a little crazy, so I told him I didn't want to lose him and well he said I would never leave you. I wanted to cry, he makes me feel so alive, different, original and well he told me I am the first girl to do this to him make him come over the phone, first off I couldn't believe I was the first but OMG that was a self esteem boost, we stay on till about 1:08 a.m. and I enjoyed every moment of it.

June 2, 1989 Friday
Dear Diary,

Well only 5 more days of school and I need a touch up on my hair and no check one way or the other I am going to get that perm well anyway me and Robert had a nice conversation, but it turned ugly he picks up an attitude and I got one too, but he thought he was doing something whatever to each as own.

June 6, 1989 Tuesday
Dear Dairy,

Well we have three more days before school is out YESSS, and well I'm going to Miss Tonya and Alisa the next three days they have already completed their time here. I have to study for my English exam in Mrs. Pollock class tomorrow 1st and 5th Period. 1st period was okay I knew mostly everything on the exam. Later on Robert called around 11:53 p.m. we talk till 4:00 a.m. but anyway we had a nice conversation it started off bad, but got a little better as we continue to talk. Robert was telling me how active he was in sex right and I was wondering how he said that he uses to do it every day until he learns to control himself and only getting it, and get this part he got tired of it (yeah right) well he also said that he can shoot off ten times in one day and well the conversation got deep and Robert ask me can I get you wet I said no, so he said I love you in the most tender way and so he said

60

getting gentle and slow with you can bring me to something more so good. He begins breathing hard, and faster and it was getting to me to hear him breath like that, but anyway he came on himself he took a shower to get the sperm off, but he told me that I'm going to turn you out I ask him what he meant and he said that I will make you want me more and you will always love me after I get you and you never leave me, I'm like WOW are you serious that's intense to think about.

June 9, 1989 Friday
Dear Diary,

Today was messy this morning it rain like cats and dogs and well me I was just chilling with everybody and so guess what as we were going to the guidance office Chris spoke to me, so anyway I pass my final in Mr. Kendrick class with an 86% and Mrs. Pollock with the something and well Mrs. Cox's class with a 80% which to me was good but I was expecting it, so after 10 seconds before the bell ring for us to end this school year it was the best, okay we trip out completely on the bus, it was fun while it lasted so after that we had to get ready for Tonya graduation it wasn't so bad, I wasn't sure if I was going to the party but I did and well Thrombi took me there and I was with John Thomas brother and so everything was cool I found Carol and hung out with her.

Let me tell you all the guys I seen today, it was Tommy Johnson, Chris Thompson, Fred Jenkins, Eric Butler, Roger Sims, Terry Willis, Wayne Miller, Kirkland Martin and his brother James. So then Tonya turned Thrombi down cold and left with Edwin, so then me and Tonya stay together until it was time to go at 2:30 a.m. so Tonya never came back so we started walking oh I seen Lank and 'em well it was Tonya, Mark and her boyfriend. We rode with the nuts so anyway I had a nice they thought I was drunk and I made them believe it too, well Earline was mad at Tonya and so was grandma for leaving me, but ole well all was good was good I slept fine.

June 10, 1989 Sat.
Dear Dairy,

Well I woke up late looking at the TV got dress and cleaned up the house for awhile and so later on Robert call but we couldn't talk that much well so we tried again around 12:57 a.m. and mama had a fit about it, but as we were talking the conversation was very a little boring and well Robert brighten it up by saying I love you over and over again and it sound so good and well I was feeling a very sharp feeling go through me so I said the same to him and he was getting a little emotional so anyway Robert said I love you so much and I told him I love you too well he told me "Terri I'm moving up and down, I'm making love to you", and I told him to stop, because I feel something and he said "well I should do it some more, so he did I love you so much but I rather not be the judge.

June 14, 1989 Wednesday
Dear Dairy,

Well today started out okay well we went to get our report card at John Johnson for Diane and she passed and me well I had to pay for a book and also no one was there at 11:38 p.m. anyway I seen Tina and we went to the mall and all look at clothes that cost a fortune and well we were talking about how ugly Mary Hamilton was and well as we were in Revco department store trying on perfume and all me and Tina were walking in Leon's and Belk's and as were in Leon's look at prices.

I saw Robert walking with Vera god that did something to me, I wanted to kill him so as I walk off they were coming in and

Dear Diary

Tina said "they were holding hands as for minute" and so he seen me and wanted to turn around but Vera got bitchy and started hugging him and well I was so mad my heart was beating fast and I was feeling dizzy with anger I wanted to hurt one of them and well he followed us through TGY, but fuck it and he had the nerve to come in my face talking shit, and I guess he thought I was happy about it and he said "I don't understand", but I understand this he best not call me okay, he got mad when I wouldn't talk to him so we went back and I didn't get my things yet, later on Craig and all of them came up about to hit me and he was acting so innocent about the shit it hurt bad and she smiling up a storm.

I wonder how Robert would have reacted if I was with another boy, I guess he want me to think of it as a friendship screw up bastard, Tina was right I'm going to go back to him like a dam fool I should've knew Robert was going to hurt me like this, I knew I just wanted to give it time but he call me nuts, but we got off at a pretty bad spot so any he told me Vera was just trying to make me mad and she succeeded so later Robert told me he never told a girl this before, but I'm begging you not to leave me and stay with me, because I don't know what would happen to me he said "please Terri don't leave me cause I love you so much and I don't want to ever let you go".

I felt guilty and I talk with Tonya and Grandma and Grandma made a lot of sense about it and what I should do and Tonya told me that she was just trying to make you mad, because I know you like Robert too much to leave him over this immature mess, I do love him and wouldn't want to leave him, well I felt a little better after that, oh I got promoted to the 11th grade YESSS, I'm a Junior I have made the best report card ever 95% in English, 79% Mr. Frazier's class, 80% in Bio, 82% in Math, 89% in Reading and finally a 84% in History WOW, so Robert call me at 12:25 a.m. and well anyway he was having an argument with Craig and he said do you want to get ill, so I said yes of course. I love him so much I don't know he make me feel so special inside and I can't

Dear Diary

help but love him back, I can't stay mad at him he makes me feel
so good inside.

June 16, 1989 Friday
Dear Dairy,

Well today was messy it started raining after I got my
application from Revco I don't know but anyway. Carol told me
the Greek show is tonight and me well I didn't go and Robert did,
but he went to the movie a well I had nice time.

I called Tina around 12:10 and well she was telling me about
the fight they had out there so then she mention how Ricky (her
boyfriend) is not longer a virgin crazy girl, but she had a good time
and Robert well I call him as soon as I got off with Tina, we got
off at a terrible start and well people were still calling after I got
off with him so after that I call him around 1:40 a.m. we talk to and
it's something about his voice well he was nice he told me that I
love you so much and I want you to always love me and well I said
something and he said that I get a temper real easy and so he was
talking up something and so then I said "Robert you are so cute
when you're mad" and I cheered him back up, he burst out
laughing and so he was talking to me and well I wanted him to
come here before he went home because I told him to but, he never
did that but anyway Robert was making me crazy inside and well I
wanted to the same to him, just thinking and hearing his voice
made me hot and well he was so soft and well it's his voice it
sound so soft tender and emotional and also it's the way he makes
me feel as I was breathing he was telling me I want you to be there
for me and he was he said if I was over there I probably just go
ahead and fuck you when I get the chance and I ask him why he
put in those terms and he said, "I am going to fuck you, but also
make love to you and make it last as long as I can, well I was still
feeling good and so he join in with me and I told him to stop
breathing like that it felt so good how he was doing it, and well as I

was getting him I was telling how good it felt and it did, I told him not to say anything and not to stop and he did, all I know was I want his dick to move up and down like he was saying and let me feel his warmth inside of me and closeness and well he is so good I really am in love (lust) with him if not I don't know it's something but I love him, and yes he love me because I look good and have a great body and a pussy of course he still the best I can ever have so then I told him I like everything about you. We started illing again and he was telling me to stop, but I didn't I kept on because well the way he was breathing made me feel good so good inside, and the way he did it sounded so cute and adorable whatever I still love what happen we got off at 3:32 a.m. and I dream it was the best thing that could ever happen to me.

June 19, 1989 Monday
Dear Dairy,

Today we start our JTPA program and our job was to work in the State Hospital just outside of Bainbridge, I was a little nervous going there but it turned out be fun while it lasted. I met some nice people especially our supervisor. They had me in a group which turned out to have fun people, along with some friends I knew. The patients at the hospital scared me half the death, but that is a fear I need to get over so I'm hoping tomorrow will turn out better and fun. Well Robert call we had a good conversation and he told me he still loved me and I've been thinking about him all day, but I still love my baby just the same.

June 21, 1989 Wednesday
Dear Dairy,

Well today was okay everybody was acting shitty and stupid look at me like I'm new or something well in class were tripping out so anyway last night I remember Robert was going to pick me

Dear Diary

up and he did him and Fred came by the classroom and well Toni said "he looks good", well anyway I was look after we left and I found him and Craig was there look nutty as ever so Robert was having a nice conversation, but I wanted to kiss him so bad, but I wasn't in the mood, well anyway at the grounds me and Robert were hug up and so my supervisor came and told us not to do that since we were still on the Hospital grounds, but other than that today was a good day.

CHAPTER 7

Bye-Bye Girl, Hello Women!
July 8, 1989 Saturday
Dear Dairy,

This is the biggest night of my life, the night I pretty much gave my virginity to Robert Thomas. Wow, where to begin as you know we have been expressing ourselves in ways that couldn't be explained. I mentioned to him how important this night was and of course he couldn't wait, Mom was working the late shift, which means I have the house completely to myself (except for my sister). It was around 9:40 pm and we were just talking and sort of making plans. Robert kept asking if I was okay with this and if I was really ready. I told him yes and that I wanted him so much. My sister passed out sleep for the night, so I told Robert he could come over, he said OKAY give me 20 min. because he was basically going to steal his brother's truck, I just hope he get here safely. I got up and nervously prepared myself; I put on a sexy black slip with nothing underneath and made myself look presentable for him.

I turned the stereo to 96.1 cause the quiet storm usually has nice soft music playing late at night. It was around 1:40 a.m. when Robert arrives, he softly taps on the door and I let him in Fife my dog started barking at him and was trying to calm her down so she wouldn't wake up my sister. Robert told me he had to park down the road so my grandma wouldn't know someone was here Nice...

I led him to the living room and he kept telling me how pretty I was and he just wanted to look at me. Robert begin to kissing and touching me all over and finally that crazy feeling came over me again in where I just wanted him, so I told him I was ready, he said "are you sure", yes Robert I am, so I led him to the guest bedroom and he proceed to caress me gently and tell me how he loved me and wanted to give me a special part of him, I mentioned this is special and I want you to have it.

While all this is going on the song from Art of Noise "A Moment in time" came on and OMG that was something else. I begin to feel relax and calm, we begin to kiss and I laid on the bed, waiting for him he begin to undress and lay next to me, still kissing and caressing my body oh so gently, finally Robert said are you ready I said yes please give it to me so finally Robert got on top of me after placing a condom on and gently massage my area till it was moist and wet and place his hard penis inside of me at first it wouldn't go in and it hurt a little so Robert slowed down to where it wasn't so bad finally a few more pushes he was there and it still hurt a little, but as he proceed it became very insatiable. I was feeling every movement and my body was accepting it all the way, after a few moments I felt like a pro I was taking Robert further inside me just to make sure this was it and WOW it was very enjoyable we completed the song and was still going at it until finally Robert let go, but we just laid there holding and caresses each other at one moment we fell asleep, Robert realized he had to take the vehicle back so we just kiss once more and he left. I quickly took a shower and just embrace what just happen; I just wanted to savor the moment instead. I was exhausted from it, but Robert called just to see how I was doing and to let me know that it was worth every bit, with that I bid good night and I'll talk with you tomorrow, but I felt so alive after that WOW.

CHAPTER 8

Leaving Robert

Robert and I had a number of sexual escapades like that over the course of our 2-year relationship. After our first encounter, I let my desires take over me. I wanted and needed more and more of him. I would let myself get carried away with my feelings; "and oh how things continue". I thought it would bring me and him closer, and it did for a moment but you can't change someone that's not ready too.

All the sexual desires I experienced were new and I let them overwhelmed me. Later, I begin to feel jealous whenever I heard of Robert talking to someone else. Keeping my virginity should've been my best decision but instead I was taken for granted without a cause. I knew Robert wasn't fully committed to me sexually, with all the rumors of him being a serial cheater and all – Robert's feelings for me were true and that's what made me happy. That was something I didn't receive, while growing up.

Some of my sexual desires for Robert took me to Dangerous places like lying to my grandma and even having sex in her house which I was disrespectful on so many levels along with skipping school, "OMG which were frequent" just to be with him.

I left Bainbridge High School the summer of my senior year because my grandma caught me and Robert together and she felt I was too much for her. I moved to Tallahassee with my Mom and sister around May 1990, where now I see was the best move for me.

I guess you are wondering; why did I live in Georgia and my Mom in Tallahassee. Well my Mom thought she could have a better life there, she purchased some land there and moved the double-wide along with my sister. She decided I should stay, since I was in the 11th grade and felt finishing up school there would be better for me. I agreed until part of my brain left my body.

This move gave me a chance to really look at what and how I was feeling for Robert. I came to realized that what I was feeling was just **lust** nothing more. Love was just words to be said but never the feelings that were truly inside me. We continued a long distance relationship and I found myself still drawn to Robert.

This lasted up to maybe after I graduated from Leon High, at that point I wasn't feeling it anymore, I saw different guys here and my point of view begin to change. The summer after I graduated from school, I let Robert Thomas go and begin a new CHAPTER with myself.

CHAPTER 9

Living in Between

Once school was behind me, I decided to live life free and explore my surroundings. Living in Tallahassee gave me plenty of options - you have FAMU, FSU and TCC with all the potential suitors in one pot just waiting for me to jump in. When I finished high school, I enrolled @ TCC for a few semesters, "honestly school was not my beckon call, I barely made it through high school hell but I had to look the part as a REAL student, plus mom was jocking me hard about doing something with myself, so in other words, I was only going just to please my Mom and not myself.

During my breaks between classes I would drive to my older cousin apartment and just chill, he attended FAMU and was a serial player. OMG the girls were always throwing themselves at him like he was a GOD or something, at one point I'm like "really, yawl think he's about you really", "of course they do", look at him, he's tall, in school, has a car & apartment and HANDSOME, shoot that was deal breaker. After watching my cousin run much game

Dear Diary

on these girls, it occurred to me, we are shallow creatures and think this is all you need in a man, but then I thought why can't I do it too, just don't catch feelings, just do me.

CHAPTER 10

Being Wild & Free

Here I begin a new CHAPTER of my life where I can call the shots and not listen to anybody. Mom gave me her car to travel to work and school, but my ass wreaked the vehicle in early '92' trying to skip class. It was late in the evening and I was should've been in class but at the last minute decided to go over my cousin's house to hang out. BIG MISTAKE, as I was leaving TCC campus and driving up Appleyard Dr. to W. Pensacola St. the light was on yellow - yellow means yield to some but to me it meant race through. While doing so a truck decided to turn left on me OMG, WHY he smashed into my driver side with such force I thought it was over. The car completely stopped and I begin to panic quickly, since the fire station was right across the street they just came out the station to where the scene was. All I could do was just sit there waiting for something to happen but nothing did just the fireman asked, "ma'am you OK", "can you exit the other side, please", I said "yeah", once done I stood for a moment collecting what just happened. The guy on the other hand was bitching that he had the right-a-way "whatever", he was cursing and complaining all the while beer cans was spilling out of his truck, dumb-ass.

The whole scene was sur-real to me, even while the EMT were assisting me I couldn't grasp what was going on. I refuse treatment and wanted to just go home. I called Malcolm, but he was busy working on a project, so I got my BF at the time and she took me home after talking w/ the tow truck driver giving me instructions on where the car will be. I didn't talk the entire time I just needed rest.

Once we reached home, I realized the keys were in the vehicle, "dammit" I had to get mom to open the door. She was wondering where's the car mindless me didn't answer just wanted to lay down. The next morning was the worse, my body reminded my ass really quick on what happened last night and OMG it was horrible, my leg was swollen and so was my entire left side of my body. I had to tell mom what happened now, cause the emergency room needed me badly. She was in shock of course of what happened, especially once she read the police report, "yeah about that", "you what had happened was" that was my story.

We visited the car to pick up the rest of my belongings and mom broke down crying, "OMG, you could've been dead", "what the hell were you thinking", "um I wasn't". That whole court thing w/ the insurance company was a drag and nothing amusing came from it.

Somewhere in the middle of summer, we begin looking for a used, mom would give half to what I had saved up to buy a she brown '86' Subaru, it needed lots of work but it was paid for and mine. I had to get car insurance since mom stated I was a risk, "man, welcome to the real world".

Finally, being an adult had more responsibilities then I realized, but I was still focus on the bigger price I was single. Since I was 19 clubs and hanging was my main priority but I still had to deal with my Mom since I was at home of course. She at least allows me freedom to do what I wanted, something I never had before. I had a group of friends that loved to go out and party and I was down with all of it. During the week, I always look forward to Friday because I knew it was on and popping.

The girls and I would plan our weekend to what club to hit, down to the clothes, it was truly a fun time in my young life, plus after working on Friday I would eagerly go home rest a little until around 10:30 p.m., I'll shower dress up and out the door by 11:15 p.m., and this is with hoping the girls, cause the club midnight deadline for girls getting in free was near.

The MOON was our spot, it wasn't a huge club, but very well known, there were events for different types of clubbers. Our nights were on Friday & Saturday, my experiences with the clubs was fun and exciting I loved to dance and be seen, but never a drinker, alcohol wasn't my speed; my friends use to pick at me religiously for not, but I had my reasons. For one, I never had a taste for it and second I didn't like being so drunk to not having functions over myself and finally I wanted to get home safe and sound. I've switched this story from living free to working the clubs, so let me get back on focus here.

One of the things I learned from my cousin was never catch feelings. I wasn't looking for a new relationship at the time I was young and at my sexual peek. I learned the rules to being a player by watching and studying him and feeling out when and how to handle certain situations. The clubs were my playground and that is where I meant most of them, they were nice and all but I just wanted to do me. My escapades were short and sweet; keeping my pager on allowed me the freedom to make sure my schedule was flexible, especially after hours from the club.

CHAPTER 11

Rules to Live By

Okay so let me skip the bull and get to the real reason for this CHAPTER on how I played the fields. I had a few basic rules I followed, but once I stepped out of bound of the rules, my player card was revoked and that wasn't cool at all. These rules help me to understand guys more, and why I wouldn't allow them to have the power. That's what it's all about girls, power you have it flaunt it. I couldn't image the heartbreak, of believing what every guy tell me, so the best defense was letting them believe me which was the easy part, the hard part Ahhh let's don't worry about that right now.

Here are some basic rules I went by to keep my heart and life free of drama.

RULE#1: Never give your phone or pager number out "that so old school" unless you want him to call, it's your option but only if you are going to keep the commitment to this particular guy if not, don't give it out.

RULE#2: Never text or friend your booty lovers on Facebook or Twitter either, that's a fine way of getting that ass in trouble and create a starker.

RULE#3: Never tell him he's the one, because they will believe it and use it against you later.

RULE#4: Always set the time and place for your escapades, remember **YOU** are in control not him.

RULE#5: Always be prepared for anything, what I mean is have your own condom stash, don't expect him to always have them, because 9 out of 10 he won't.

RULE#6: Next, don't give him too much in the bedroom, that's a sure way of keeping his ass calling, but again only if you want him too.

RULE#7: When a guy says he can rock your world, dare him and when he lies about it, drop his ass and go on, no harm no fowl.

RULE#8: Never keep going back to the same one more than once; cause then feelings start kicking in and your trap. That's the worst position to be in especially when you are not ready.

Last, don't get with guys from the club, you will have an awesome night, but don't expect that fool to be your boyfriend later, remember you meant him at the club, enough said. During my new and wild life, I ran into a few people that had me feeling myself.

I remember this one guy I meant at the club name Derrick, we exchanged numbers talked a couple of times, before we meant up later in the week for a booty call, which by the way was exciting. I admit it was fun but I gave the brother too much of myself, cause then going back to *rule # 4*, this fool appeared at my job asking for a quickie talking about *"I'm missing that ass"*, *"you're crazy bro, not on my job"*, nope he was dead serious and demanded another date, at this point I knew I fuck up on *rule #6*, so I had to let him go.

Now one thing about me was I was a hit it and quit it girl, I had escapades with several guys that only lasted that night and the reason for that. I was a picky girl and wanted to be satisfied, if he couldn't do it the first time, then sorry boo I don't give second chances. I felt empowered using my sexuality to the fullest, not limiting myself to just one. I didn't consider myself a teacher, so why should I teach a guy how to fuck; he should know that before getting with me, right. Yes, you can say I was a cocky girl but when it came to getting mine, why not. I hated for a guy to challenge me in the bedroom, it was really interesting to see what they could do and if he comes up short, I'm done, don't call, page or text me just know it was a night and tomorrow is another day. There were guys that were sweet, the problem was I was damage goods and didn't want the mushy stuff.

Now I know you guys are thinking "really no guy was good enough for her", I didn't say that, there was a time I almost lost my player card over some good ass dick; he was different in a sort of special way.

Tommy was the popular guy around T-Town driving his Ford Explorer "yes I did say Ford Explorer this was early "90" so they were big back then" he always kept it fresh and oh he was a cutie. I meant him in the club one night after Dancing with my friends, he wanted to holla I guess after staring at him so much it was only natural. He asked for my number and I gave my pager number just to see would he call, cause all the girls at the club was near him, like he was a celebrity or something.

After a few days he called and it was on and popping. I saw him during one of FAMU's home games and me and my girl was just cruising the strip trying to be seen, Tommy drove by and saw me and pop this look like "girl what's up", I smiled and kept on driving, next thing I know, he made a U-turn and demanded I get in, with no hesitation I parked side the road with the car still running and my girl inside and bounce.

Once I got in, he parked the truck with no time to spare and I pounce on him and was finished in time, before my friend could get worry, see that's what I'm talking about unexpected ass, it can come at any time or place and you have to be prepared for *rule #5* ladies. I kept messing with Tommy a few times more, which draws me to *rule #8* I lost myself in Tommy. I was beginning to think we were a couple, due to the time he was spending with me. The fatal blow came, after seeing Tommy with another girl, I was actually jealous that's where I messed up at trying to be nice.

I couldn't believe I was catching feeling for this guy what the hell. I had to fall back and regroup myself and understand it was all for fun, nothing personal. So with that, I found myself many times questioning why was I here, or doing things I knew weren't right. After taking a Moment to reevaluate my life and the things I was doing, I decided to change; the next person I meet would need to be special. This is where Malcolm came in.

CHAPTER 12

Finding Malcolm

Meeting Malcolm Wallace was like a breath of fresh air to know someone like him even existed was amazing. The summer of '92 was the bomb year. I was fresh out of high school and was just living life to the fullest. I begin working that summer at a Printing Company full time, which my Mom got for me after I was let go from McDonald's. She wanted me to continue to pay rent "yes I said it, rent to stay at home".

While there I met this guy name Bradley Walker, he was a tall big guy with a nice personally whom I could just sit and joke with. Bradley was a student at FAMU and just working part-time for some pocket change, for some reason I was drawn to him, it was nice to have someone around to make me laugh and make the day go faster. After, getting to know him, we begin to hang out with a few of his friends. Once day my friend Fay and I went by his place on a Friday afternoon just to hang out with him and the boys, Joe and Tony.

That evening I meant the father of my future kids and husband to be. Malcolm was coming in after work dressed in a white shirt, blue tie with black slacks to match looking extra cute. I was speechless which is unusual for me, but he took my breath away. All I could do was stare at him, it was like we were alone in the room it seems like eternity, Bradley and the others started calling me names and what not, but my attention was totally on him, "like WOW he's a cutie".

After that awkward Moment I was ready to go, after excusing myself from his place, I begin bragging to my friend about him, OMG what can become of us. We were acting like middle aged school girls over again.

Here I'm beginning a new CHAPTER only talking about Malcolm my future husband and father to my children. At the beginning it was awkward, we were both out of relationships and just wanted to be friends, well that's what he wanted. I had an agenda for him and friends was one, but I wanted to add boyfriend to that list as well. What Mr. Malcolm needed to understand is; when my mind is set up for something I will stop at nothing to get it, so if he wants to be friends WHATEVER we can play that game, but I knew what was really going down.

During my time getting to know Malcolm, I jolted down my time with him in my infamous diary, explaining every detail of our friendship/hook ups. I was very fond of this time, it was different from Robert it showed I was in desperate need of companionship and love something I lacked in my life and he provided that all in one pot. Malcolm gave me life, meaning and understanding. So let's being my tales.

Nov 30, 1992, Monday
Dear Diary,

Today I felt special, last night my baby (current boyfriend) finally came home after being gone for 2-weeks visiting family. When I heard his voice I felt at ease with myself; I told him how much I missed him and wanted to be with him. When I first met him I knew there could be something between us, Kris Cromartie maybe not all I want but he's the first guy since Robert I've said I love you too after last night.

I never thought in a couple of years would I say that to anyone else, but I did. I think about him all the time and well he's nice I guess I love him like I did Robert, but I can't hurt myself like I did with him, all he did was cause me pain, I just pray and hope Kyle is different. Last night we talk about everything I somehow care about this guy a lot, but I'm afraid to admit it.

Feb 21, 1993, Sunday
Dear Diary,

This guy that I know name Malcolm Willis, I really like and adore a lot, well he's a very respectful young intelligent guy, he's 24 yrs old and a graduate from FAMU. I've talked to him a couple of times over the phone, and maybe I could ask him out. Malcolm agreed to go out with me and I was on cloud nine until later on that night around the time it's for us to go, and he called to cancel. I felt disappointed about it, even angry and then maybe it was someone else or he just didn't want to be with me. I felt bad he really couldn't say much to me about it nor could he apologize for it. I'm a little hurt over this and I'm wondering should I not call or talk to him, but that's not how my mind work; I have to find out why he backed out on me. It took me months, before I could ask him out and after being rejected I wasn't the same.

Maybe Malcolm doesn't realize how much I really care for him and that everything I have said and express to him I can't take it back nor how I feel I keep saying maybe because I'm too young or have short hair or maybe not attractive enough. Malcolm is the guy I always wanted to be with, and now well I feel like I deserve an explanation to what happened. I should also tell him how I feel and how I put aside so many people just to try to get myself situated with him.

April 11, 1993, Sunday
Dear Diary,

Something about Malcolm has change for one when I talk to him now the conversations now are lively. I love talking to him because then I'll feel better afterwards. He seems more eager to talk, at first when I started talking to him I just wanted to have sex, but after getting to really now him I've become to understand that I could have a friendship with him instead of sex. I feel now that if he makes the first move I may hesitate or I may just go for it.

April 18, 1993 Sunday
Dear Diary,

I finally went on a date with Malcolm it was like a dream. All that day I kept anticipating our date, and I didn't share the news with anyone until it happened, I felt embarrassed about the last date that didn't happen. First I figured we were going to eat, so I wore a dress instead and well he had on shorts when I came over he looked so cute sitting up there, we went to Subway and I had a 6" tuna and he a 12" tuna sub we went to the park and ate there and enjoyed the scenery just me and him. After the date, I couldn't wait to call my friend to explain the date and what happened, it was so cool to just hang out with him and not think only about sex.

CHAPTER 13

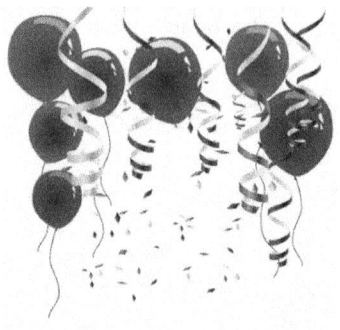

The Waiting is Finally Over
June 7, 1993, Monday
Dear Diary,

I finally got what I've been waiting six months for, having some kind of physical contact with Malcolm. Finally, at first he was talking to his roommate and all I thought maybe he would be alone oh well I know I was happy to be with him.

At first we were just looking at TV and all and then he started playing with it. Anyhow I was doing something and he grab me and kiss me, I pulled away thinking was going to play with my mind again. Anyhow I didn't wear a bra under my romper so he kept looking at them like what's up anyhow he begins sucking on them and teasing them like he's crazy, but it felt nice very nice. I even encourage him, afterwards he stops and then he mentions I'm making you upset aren't I. I told him yes and you know how much I want you, so well I started messing with the TV again and he just turned it off, and begin bothering my breasts again, this time he was taking me to the limits. I lay back on the chair and I just ask Malcolm to come over here now, he did after I asked twice. I mention to him next time I call you better come, and then he begins getting a little crazy with me. He then said "what you want to happen now" like he didn't know. So I played dumb and said "what you think" so he said, "let me get some protection" I like no I have some so then it was on.

Malcolm was putting on the condom while I was undressing I guess I wasn't fast enough for him he helped. Well anyways he was on top, and changed his mind and wanted me on top on his lap. I did at first and it was this sharp pain at first and then it felt real nice. I was trying my best to give Malcolm everything I had, something happens and well he apologizes for going back limp and I didn't even though I was a little upset. Afterwards we were back to normal looking at TV, I admit I loved every minute of it, but I guess because I liked this it was sort of hard to start talking to him. He asked a question that to this day I can't answer, he said "were you in some sort of athletic sports" I mentioned I ran track for 2 years, I asked him why he never answered, later he was trying to fall asleep on me so I decided to leave after walking out of his apartment we said a couple of things to each other and before I say goodbye he left. I felt kind of crazy, but I guess this is what I asked for. I hope we could do this again some more. My feeling for Malcolm hasn't change, but I would like for us to have uncontrollable sex one entire night.

July 13, 1993 Sunday
Dear Diary,

Church was nice me and mama went and enjoyed a good service even though my mind was on afterwards; I was going to the mall with Lonnie and Joy. I brought two outfits and wanted a pair of shoes but my money was funny anyhow.

I called Malcolm and we were just tripping and all and I reminded him that we were to see each other anyhow he came over and well he bought some subway sandwiches, which were crazy and all, I never really got into Subway until I meant Malcolm but it was a change I wouldn't regret.

I took Malcolm to our local park and we just talked, after I didn't eat the sandwich he brought me we left he asked me did he want to take me home I said no I just wanted to be with him. I thought maybe Malcolm would take me somewhere else, but he took me back to his apartment to watch "Coming to America" was on and well were tripping on the movie, it was getting to the part of the movie where they figure Eddie out he was the Prince and Malcolm start approaching me and begin kissing on me; I respond fully. I enjoyed every Moment, every kiss and touch we ever had was worth it.

Then Malcolm stood turned the light off and begin unbutton my jumper, me or course well I asked him was he trying to tease me half the death, but when I look again he was putting on a condom and then he help take off my clothes and well Malcolm was on me before I could say anything. It felt so nice to be with him it was one position that I have never been in that drove me slap crazy, it was like a stand up position in where my legs were wrap around his body OMG it was like heaven to me, but then I guess he got tired of standing like that he sat me down at the edge of the stair case and was still steady going.

Malcolm really didn't want me to make any kind of effort for me to please him, so I just enjoyed it. I felt I had come earlier, but I couldn't tell. Malcolm finally told me he was about to come, God I couldn't wait he did and it felt so joyous for the both of us. I always figure Malcolm could be a very good lover, but to be truthful that's the first time I ever enjoyed sex to the extreme like that. Robert couldn't top that if he tried, afterwards I was in shock to how good he was that I quickly excuse myself to take a shower. I felt that Malcolm wanted more, but I was sore from that experience.

Dear Diary

I figured after being away for two-weeks that maybe he felt he had to get his release we begin to talk and all but when I ready to head home he kiss me good night it felt very nice.

July 21, 1993 Saturday
Dear Diary,

Today at work it was very hard and boring, but I was looking forward to tonight. I made up some crazy story about leaving work when I approached Malcolm's house he wasn't there until later at that time I was getting very disappointed very, but after stopping at Ron's house I called Malcolm to come over and I did anyhow Malcolm was looking good as ever and fine he had a nice little ass there.

Anyhow, I was still mad I started hitting him like I was crazy and all, oh well after listening to his explanation for not being home I got upset again and started hitting him again after him tripping so I sat down beside him and just enjoyed the movie "Boomerang" anyhow he starts kissing on me and I told him to stop, but later we were back at it again this time it was getting intense so well I let up and said something about checking to see if his roommate was asleep.

He came along messing with me again, but this time driving me crazy, well Malcolm really had me wet so he gently pulled my shorts off and he begin inserting the condom on. So far I was looking then he was I guess trying to force himself inside me, because it was painful at first I wanted to say something, but I held back, afterwards the pain turn to pleasure it was the most delightful feeling I ever felt.

Malcolm mention he was coming I told him not to because I wasn't ready, he said he couldn't help it later after he came I still held on to him and mention to him not to get up he said he won't and he felt so warm and nice. After that we dress and I felt rejected, because I wanted to go further than that. Anyhow we begin to talk and I wanted to know how he felt about me he said that he liked me a lot, but he didn't feel any love for me. He said I was someone he enjoys talking to and a very nice person. I told him that I care for him deeply and he said he cared about me too. I begin joking around with him and all and well I just enjoyed feeling and holding him that I forgot time I just wanted to stay with him all night and day, I will be seem not interested in me leaving I stayed until 1:30 A.M. realizing how late it was.

I want Malcolm in a relationship I'll do what I have do to have him. He's handsome, fine, intelligent, caring and respect oh and very skillful at making love, like I said before I never had anyone as pleasing as him. We hug and kiss and said our good –byes which is normal for friends, but I'm going to keep for the better maybe one day he will see things my way.

July 31, 1993 Saturday
Dear Diary,

Well I spent all Sat. at Lonnie's store, because I told mama I was going to work, anyhow I went to work later after hanging with her, anyhow I came home quickly after hearing I got my Express and AT&T card, it's shopping time. I wanted to go to the mall and well after getting in touch with Yolanda she went with me and bought a 2-piece outfit with a silk blouse with it, which came to a total of $164.99 whew too much. I wanted to plan an evening with Malcolm so I called him around 9:00 P.M. to let him know I was coming over. I packed a few of my clothes and well I headed over feeling good and all, well I mentioned to him that I wanted to talk to him so we went to the park.

It was fun telling him my problems and listening to him we stayed there close to an hour but we didn't. So well after getting something to eat and returning back to his apartment we started tripping out about who and what we were going to look at anyhow I slap him with the pillow and we begin playing around with each other and he was killing me with his weight anyhow we kept messing around until he became seriously and start kissing me anyhow I was enjoying every breathing Moment of it Malcolm mentioned he didn't have protection so I told him I do, well anyhow me and Malcolm were getting very intimate when he couldn't get himself right on the chair anyhow he ask did I want to go upstairs I said ya, well anyhow we did and Malcolm had a problem at first, but then he entered I was so relieved it felt so good to have him well afterwards I took a shower and begin to put on my pajamas and well tried to be cocky and well he said well the young generation sure wear pajamas out, anyhow Malcolm call himself sleeping and I kept fucking around with him, because I wanted to have sex again, so well every time I touch his private parts until he knew he couldn't resist. So it was on again Malcolm felt so nice and when we change over it was not so good but pleasurable.

Afterward I felt sleepy so I felled asleep, anyhow someone called at 7:20 P.M. and they wanted to come over and well I had to go Malcolm was nice about it he requested answering the phone but I didn't mind, but I had a wonderful time as always.

August 14, 1993 Saturday
Dear Diary,

I've been very boring sitting around the house doing nothing but chilling. I thought about Malcolm all day and every time I've never been in a friendship situation like the one I'm in now. I can talk to him about my problems and he'll listen, but the problem I'm having and how to deal with them, having sex with someone that I already care very deeply about him.

Anyhow I truly just wanted to sex him after two months of teasing and seven months of waiting something finally happens it felt so wonderful to be in his arms I just love the way he makes me feel and the sex is awesome I never had anyone to make me feel way. Malcolm made me feel the fact still reminds me how I feel about Malcolm has driven me deep within myself, I just wish our friendship could become deep we had sex four times.

Aug. 23, 1993 Monday
Dear Diary,

I found where Bradley and Tony were staying with their new roommate name Mike he's a cutie, but he's not nothing like my baby Malcolm, speaking of him after spending an hour and so over Bradley house I called Malcolm and said could I have an hour of your time, he said yes so I went over there and well Malcolm looked so cute sitting up there with those dinky shorts on and all. He later took a bath for what reason I don't and well anyhow Malcolm wanted to know the reason for me being there I told him that basically to visit, not telling him.

Well anyhow we sat on the couch and he said how nice my hair was, Sa put his arm around me and I jerk it off he grab me and well we kiss, but he said something that made me upset so I call Diane to let her know I was on my way I was about to leave and on my way upstairs he came up on me real close kissing and caressing me, I could feel his hardness, so I said "fine Malcolm don't start and it won't be nothing" I begin walking up the stairs and he was patting my behind and he kiss me very deeply and it was nice and that's when he begin to unbutton my bra I knew I wasn't leaving, after letting go he said "I'll be twenty minutes or three" anyhow he was guiding me into his room I kiss and hug him until we laid on the bed. Malcolm was very nice I ask him about the music and he proceed to turn it on anyhow Malcolm came back by then I had undress, and Malcolm well he gently laid me down and was on top and begin kissing me anyhow it hurt a little when Malcolm begin to move in and well afterwards it begin to feel very good, I wish I could fake it with him, but I can't it really did feel good and well Malcolm was kissing me while having sex it was a first anyhow

Malcolm begin to come and well I held on to him it felt so deep to be there and felt so alive afterward while Malcolm was still inside me I mention to him that I feel better now, he started laughing and begin telling me some crazy story about the film, anyhow Malcolm was still in the same position in which I guess he was enjoying it.

After talking for a while he released which left me moaning about that time, at that Moment I was getting dress in front of Malcolm who was looking, he should know by now that he's the only person that I'm doing. I figured the reason why I was hurting like that because it's been a month, sex with Malcolm is heaven he feels so good and so warm it's never weak sex but exciting incredible fulfilling sex.

Sept 2, 1993 Thursday
Dear Diary,

Well work was very busy at the Cleaners, today was tense because Linda somehow got Rosie to turn against me like she come at me talking all loud and shit, people like her will never have peace of mind with themselves or anyone else, and that's a different story in a different time. Nothing about today stood out just wanted to work my shift and go home.

Sept 3, 1993 Friday
Dear Diary,

Today I spent it being mama's little taxi driver, taking her everywhere and all well anyhow I just didn't want to stay home anymore. I called everyone and they weren't home so I had to leave anyhow I pass Malcolm's apartment and he was there, so I went to Burger King and called him from the pay phone and asked if I could come over and he said yes, at first I had to see the new club that just came out on Apalachee Parkway called the "H" it was some classy, but yet hip club for the Grown & Sexy over 21, afterwards I went in Malcolm's apartment and his roommate was there she was in a cheerful mood which surprise me.

Malcolm was looking very adorable lying on the couch. So well it was this movie that was on called "The Clock" it was about a clock taking over a house, after that his roommate came tripping about a news brief special in where a man was shot seven times before dying, she begins talking about how she would shoot them and the justice system was messed up, anyhow after she ate and all and dip upstairs. Malcolm of course kept fucking with the TV anyhow I begin bothering with him after he wouldn't let my arm loose I took his watch instead he claim that I wasn't leaving with it, but um whatever, so I told him to come closer I did and well he unfasten my bra and begin rubbing my breasts like he's crazy and all and well I kiss him and it was wonderful anyhow he seem like he wanted more than that so well Malcolm told me he'll be right back well he did and was at me before you know it well he slid right in no problem what so ever and it felt so nice it always feel good to be with Malcolm anyhow he came and it was nice anyhow I choose not to get dress because something may happen again so well we watch this show and it was tripping so then I decided to put on my clothes and I was getting ready to leave anyhow before leaving I kiss him and well he looked so adorable standing there I kiss him again and hug him after leaving I realize I still had his watch on so I turn around and bought it back. I felt really good all that night.

Sept 13, 1993 Monday
Dear Diary,

Well anyhow I got my pay check and put a down payment on some insurance which is Emerald Coast mama wanted me to bring her something to eat and I did just to keep her off my back, anyhow I called Malcolm for some off the wall excuse to see him, but well when I approached his apartment and I guess he figured I was going to come in but I just wanted to get the screw driver and go anyhow I went on in and he had the living room looking a hot mess, I kept looking at TV talking to him and well he was complimenting me on how cute I looked and all I thought was how sweet. I mentioned to him how awful he looked with his rugged hair on his face and head. So he grabs and begin shaking me and well he turned and hug me and it hurt my breasts and I told him it hurt and punch him, but then I apologized for hitting him like that.

I begin chit-chatting with him after I begin slapping on him and all, I kiss him with all I had until the passion became so intense to where Malcolm asked me did I have any type of protection I said no, and he replied to let him check. I felt silly waiting like I did and well he came back and he begin kissing me again this time emotionally I felt a surge go through me and well he begins undressing me and we were at it again this.

Well anyhow we begin and well it was beginning to hurt a little but later feel very pleasurable I really wish we could go another position because this is beginning to crap my style greatly. Afterwards he'll dress and act like that at one point I was ready to go anyhow, Malcolm was following and he hug me and kiss me a couple of times, as if he didn't want me to leave, but um I'm still attracted to Malcolm, but I was very scared to I feel about him seriously. What makes me feel the way I do about him hasn't changed, he's different from the guys I've known, Malcolm is very interesting and I kind of like that very much. I never wanted anything to happen to Malcolm or try to hurt him. I hope he feels the same about me and that he wouldn't try to hurt me.

Sept. 16, 1993 Friday
Dear Dairy,

Malcolm and I had our first argument I guess I wanted to see him and well I did and Malcolm well he was in a discussion over a TV program anyhow I felt a little discussed about the way they have treated this death over the tourist incident, well Malcolm of course was a little into it, and suddenly he got real quiet then all of a sudden I said "well Malcolm you talk a little and everything and well he got mad and said "well I told you that I was studying and he got real upset I said okay then I tried to explain myself, but as I was leaving he just slam the door like okay but as I got home I called and apologize for something I shouldn't well he apologize and all but I still felt a little sad about the situation.

Sept 17, 1993 Sat.
Dear Diary,

I care so much about Malcolm, I never wanted to hurt him in anyway so I thought maybe I should just stay away from him because I feel like I'm going to get hurt really bad if I keep talking and making passionate or just plain sex with Malcolm.

I wanted to be with him in more ways than one, but it's getting to a point where I don't know what I and Malcolm have. I don't want to make him upset or get annoyed with me like he was last night. I wish I could just sit and talk to him about my feeling and not hurt myself just holding it inside. I know I'm not the one for Malcolm but I wish he would give me a chance to prove myself to him. I just want to express myself to him tell him how much I love being with him and how he holds, kiss and just be with me he was or is the most important part in my life right now I always thought Malcolm as a special person in my life even when the first time I met him he's just the one for me. I hate I have to be treated life dirt or feel unattached when I'm around or with Malcolm.

Sept. 24. 1993 Friday
Dear Diary,

Work was long and boring I called Malcolm a couple nights before for us just to chill together you know, well I got home around 6:30 and mama well she was talking about leaving town for the weekend anyhow I was eager to be with him after buying this outfit, so well I called Malcolm to see what's up he was tripping about he couldn't come and get me so I had to drive over to his house and well I rented "Dracula" to look at well they were into the T.V. him and his roommate, it was a report about a lady who cut her husband's penis off and well Malcolm's roommate and him got into it about that shouldn't happened for no one like that well this went until Malcolm realize he couldn't get him point through, so well I ask Malcolm did he have any popcorn he said no and did I want to go to the store with him well at that time we did and instead bought Taco's and made it back.

During the movie Malcolm kept saying is somebody going to die I told him no not yet, so well after the movie we just chilled and my breast were sore and he begin rubbing them but in the wrong spot also I kiss him just to be doing it. So I laid next to him on the sofa he felt so warm and well I turned and begin kissing him deeply and I put everything into those kisses and much, much more it was getting pretty intense in where I was getting a little crazy with him as well, then he wanted to go further I was on top and it wasn't painful, but it felt real hard, every time he pumped in and out it was so unfeeling for me that I told him to switch because it was feeling uncomfortable well we did and it felt a little better I couldn't wait for Malcolm to come he did and I felt exhausted he went into the bathroom and I of course went for a cup of water Malcolm came out and I was standing against the counter when he kissed me on the neck I guess he figured I was tired because he ask me did I want to go lay down on his bed I said yes of course , but I wanted to take a shower to get clean up a little better oh well. I did and I felt 100% FRESHER. Malcolm had on this top and bottom and I ask for the top of his pajamas instead he gave them to me freely with no problems we talked and later dose now I woke up at 8:30 AM because I wanted to leave at 9:00 AM. I had to be at work at around 11:30 so well he looks, even better in the morning,

I thought oh he so cute, but after walking out the door I wanted to hug him but I didn't.

Sept. 25, 1993 Saturday
Dear Diary,

When I wanted to spend time with Malcolm I called him and well he couldn't come over because he wanted to attend church the next day. Malcolm mention how spiritual he wants to be into the bible mentally and sexual, I was a little confuse over what he was saying to me did that mean he wanted to stop having sex until he got married. Well I thought maybe I wanted to know what's up between me and him well he said he kind of understood how I felt and that he didn't want to stop just yet. I was beginning to enjoy him more and more and I'm also falling for him I feel so close to him very close I care so much about and when Malcolm ask me how did I feel about him I wanted to tell Malcolm I love him very much but not long, I told him everything we had a close but nice conversation with him now I feel a little better knowing that he thinks of him as a flank which is not true he's very supportive and giving of his time and body. I told Malcolm that I was acting different sort of changing my attitude with everything trying to be what I thought he wanted me to be.

Oct 2, 1993 Saturday
Dear Diary,

Well work was crazy it was busy from 10:30 to 6:00 PM, and well I was happy to be gone. Anyhow I got home and Diane was still here and well I was wondering why and well she said mama said I could go out, anyhow it was around 7:30PM when I called Malcolm and he wasn't home I was feeling a little upset with Malcolm when I couldn't get in contact with him well any how I was feeling blue very upset until I called Tonio and well he tried t cheer me up, but somehow there was a beep and well it was Malcolm of course he was concern wanting to know why was I acting like I was anyhow he was still forward for tonight, but um I still wanted to be mad and stuff. I put on my best threads and well I looked so cute and well Malcolm did come we left and headed back to his apartment any how we begin looking at the video tape of Jade and well he cooked some popcorn which was to greasy anyhow his roommate came down and was cleaning the kitchen and bathroom and Malcolm came over and he sat next to me and held me anyhow he kissed me and was been very affectionate while his roommate was there anyhow after she departed well he became very affectionate he begin rubbing and kissing my breasts ever so gently anyhow we were getting deep until the phone rang and it was for him, anyhow whatever the conversation was about he had to leave for a Moment and I kissed him, well when he came back he wanted to go for it and he kept tucking at my suit, so I told him no Malcolm my period is on he was like OKAY and it seem like his whole attitude changed, but he still held me and I got very frisky with him even though he couldn't do anything so well we played around hug and kissed until it was getting late so Malcolm suggest I stayed over and I leave and be home by 6:30 P.M. we went to lay down and Malcolm ask me did I want a top and I said no and well I just laid there until he finished and I started playing well I wanted to be in his arms but um I kind of spilled my guts and I didn't really tell him that he's the only one that has been satisfying me to the fullest with me sexuality. He smiled and kissed me and I also wanted to know why he thought of himself as a flank anyhow he didn't want to crush me by holding me so he said, let me turn over and it was off to sleep when 6:20 came around he woke me and well I step to the bathroom to look decent, and we left. When we approach my crib well I unlock the door and turned around and hug and kiss Malcolm goodbye I care so much about.

Dear Diary

October 9, 1993 Saturday
Dear Dairy,

Well anyhow Miami loss to FSU and well work was okay it
wasn't much going on there, but um Yolanda wanted to go out and
I wanted to see Malcolm also well I had to make a choice on who I
wanted to see so I choice Malcolm anyhow I didn't want to leave
Diane by herself so well I made up some lie to get with him and I
did and he was studying so I didn't do too much but just look and
all at TV, anyhow Malcolm kept staring at me like he wanted
something anyhow I wanted something sweet so well I went and
got a cooler out the fridge and I drank it up so well I told Malcolm
this isn't an alcoholic beverage he told me it is so well I felt tipsy
from it and well Malcolm was picking at me and he came over and
kiss me and told me I need hook on phonics he just kept fucking
with me on that so we begin kissing and all and playing around
anyhow he begin teasing sucking the hell out of my breasts and his
roommate was on the phone and it seem like she was coming down
stairs I told Malcolm to stop anyhow he ask me did I want to go
upstairs anyhow we did and Malcolm was back at it he turned off
the lights and turn on some music and I took off my clothes and
laid out on the bed and well waited Malcolm slowly climb on top
of me and begin inserting it was painful at first maybe because I
was tensing up I tried to relax but I guess I couldn't anyhow
Malcolm begin to feel nice afterwards but I silent my moans to a
minimum because I didn't want his roommate to hear so well
every stroke was feeling so nice and I felt so alive under him. I
wanted nothing but too just hold him and mad the sex was
awesome well Malcolm was coming and he was making noise and
I told him to hush and well he just lay in my arms.

I wanted to just stay there I asked him how did he feel and he
said fine and he ask me the same I told him I couldn't describe it,
after he released he took a shower afterwards I did the same and
well after the shower his roommate came out and well I didn't

know whether to go stay of course I dip back into his room Malcolm was laughing and all I wasn't OKAY I uncomfortable with her being there ever though that's his roommate still, so well I put on my clothes as if I was ready to go and Malcolm was like you're ready to go now huh I said no not true anyhow.

Oct. 26, 1993 Tuesday
Dear Diary,

Last night I had a very interesting talk with Malcolm. I went by to give him my money when I approached his apartment and well anyhow I begin to knock and I thought about the money that had left in the car but as soon as I came back he was standing there anyhow I went towards him giving him the money and he ask me what was wrong I told him nothing then he grab me and told me to come inside so I did and he hug me well I didn't respond and he really thought I had a problem.

So well after talking briefly with Diane I looked at Malcolm and told him to come downstairs so we could talk I told Malcolm that my hateful feelings for men about how I was raised and that our conversation last Sunday was a party where you were telling me how many partners you have now and you said two, he claimed that's not what he said he thought when the last six months. So he told me not right now it's just me, I wanted to smile, but I had to be a lady.

After telling him that and getting a better understanding of everything Malcolm finally express to me that he cares for me and like to continue the way he feels for me too. I wanted so much as to hug him anyhow I begin messing with this paper while he was on the phone, I felt foolish but I can't let my guard down for anything, because I hate to get hurt I love being with him and everything afterwards I hugged and kiss him. At the time when I was leaving we were fooling around. I begin hugging him so

Dear Diary

tightly I just didn't want to let him go and I asked him could we be together on this weekend.

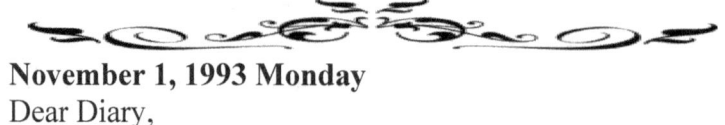

November 1, 1993 Monday
Dear Diary,

Today seems so long work was busy my car started up it was very cold today. Anyhow I wanted to see Malcolm so well I went to my boys' house Bradley and talk to them and Malcolm well I ask could I come over and well he said yes so well I get over there and well he want to play pleasure with me I hold him and all and he wants to play with me so I got bad and well begin playing around with him telling him that I'm leaving after he kept leaving me downstairs like that. I kept wondering am I pushing you or what so I grab him and pulled him on top of me and held him there and well he grab me and begin kissing me like crazy and I was loving it of course anyhow he asked me did I want to go upstairs in his room and I said yeah so well he shut the door and begin kissing me as well as undressing me it felt nice so I laid on the bed as he pulled my jeans down and so he insisted the condom and begin coming in well I told him that it will hurt well it didn't he told it shouldn't it felt so good to hold him and feel him.

Malcolm I miss you and well he didn't say anything but I kept saying all I could to get him to respond to me even though he wouldn't respond to me I felt rejected and also foolish anyhow Malcolm was pumping and putting me in crazy uncomfortable positions and well I told him to stop anyhow he was saying do it feel good I told him no not knowing what he was saying so I kept saying no then I turned around and said yes after really listening to him, then I said yes, yes baby it does feel good and well later Malcolm came I was happy afterwards he pulled out and laid on top of me, I love it more than anything Malcolm was very good and so very good and so you filling. He seems like he was going to sleep, but I awoke him and well I told him to wake up and so

102

well he went to the bathroom to take the condom off and clean up well he came back and Malcolm laid next to me I begin hugging and holding Malcolm because I love just being feeling his body with mine. Well he asked what time did I want to leave I said at 5:30 he woke me about 4:30 and I got up dress and was out the door and well I felt very good hugging him goodbye.

November 5, 1993 Friday
Dear Diary,

Well work fun and boring anyhow mama pick me up for work and we headed home anyhow my car is still sick and Yolanda isn't I guess to see her mama well Cedric called to see if we could go out, but to be truthful I don't want to so well I left a message for Malcolm hoping he'll get it knowing he wouldn't care. Well I start thinking about Malcolm he doesn't give a damn about me. I can't let my guard down, because of how I feel about him. Many reasons why I shouldn't believe Malcolm didn't give a damn about me is when, he only calls when he wants something or when he things something is wrong, next like when I called Malcolm to be with him just for that night he turns me away like I'm sort of a fool or something he doesn't want to be around me. I feel like I'm alone with him like nothing matters to him he knows I like him and would close to do anything for him but yet he doesn't care or give a damn about me, like the time when I was mad at him he made it seem life hey let me apologize because that's free pussy I'm giving up and I told Malcolm and every other guy I don't want to be played nor fucked over especially with my feelings.

When I told Malcolm I miss him at the time we were making love or having sex he didn't respond so of course my instinct kick in and I figured hey this mother-fucker just getting with me because I kept pressuring him. I hate to be used by anybody and I feel Malcolm is using my feelings to get his way something I'm just this little ass girl who wants to get with him well I feel he doesn't care if I just stop calling or decide to see someone else. I hate to be foolish here, but I want to know what is so honorable about me that I can't get with him one minute he's with me and next he can't stand me I am not going to go through the motion to finding out his dam problem if the highly educated mother-fucker don't want to have anything to do with I suggest he forget me or least tell me.

I'm tired of crying sleepless nights and wondering if he sleeping with someone else late at night or using I to be this second pussy slap bitch on the side. I'll feel better if I don't bother anybody for a long period of time. I'm not sorry for falling for Malcolm I care very deeply for him but I hate he thinks of me even though he claims he cares it doesn't faze me a bit, I still care for him but I wish he would tell me the truth on why he doesn't want to spend time with me or why it kills him to even take me out I feel like some criminal only be seen with her at your apartment only I may be young but not stupid not at all if a guy such as Malcolm doesn't want to have anything to do with me well they all can go to hell.

November 8, 1993 Monday
Dear Diary,

Today I didn't go to work or get a check so well I just chilled until my car started and well I wanted to take it to the shop to be check out but I too lazy, so I called Malcolm to let him now I was coming over anyhow when I got there Malcolm was being very noble and all I sat down to explain my reasons for asking him about if he would follow me to this place called "The Tuning Point" so I could leave my car overnight and well I look up at Malcolm and well he kept giving excuses like he didn't want to.

So I told him to forget it and well he was behind me and begin hugging and holding me, so well we started looking at T.V. and I was position him between my legs just to hold his neck so well

Dear Diary

Jaime Foxx was on again so we watch that and after it went off, "Cemetery 2" came on and I asked Malcolm could we go and well we did and he let me drive his car to a phone booth so I could drive back to his house and spend the night, so he took off my clothes to put on his robe top anyhow we looked at something and I was getting sleepy so I took both of the blankets mines and his and headed upstairs and well he kept up and well he laid down and I climb on top of him and begin bothering him and he was rubbing my behind so I kissed him and he felt something and so did I he begin moving up n down on me with his body and begin gently pulling my panties off, and he mentioned he didn't have a condom so well I told Malcolm I have some so I gave him mine, but he seem reluctant to take it so we kept on kissing and rubbing each other when he begin kissing and licking my breasts I had a fit and that's when he wanted the condom so I gave it to him and after he put it on It was on and it felt solo good very good that I didn't want it to end but I must was feeling pretty good because he is getting pretty wild and was kissing my lips and face like crazy I then got real wild and he was accepting it, but I asked did he want to turn over her said yes and it was good. I never felt like I did with anyone I told Malcolm he felt so good and well he told me you too, so something happened with the condom and it hurt so I threw my legs in some crazy position so Malcolm jump up and I asked him did the condom bust so after I bathe and returned he was so cute laying there I was a little sad after that so well Malcolm asked me what's the matter I told him that I was concerned about the condom I really don't want to screw it up for him or myself I have never cared for someone so much like I do about Malcolm later we talked and I turned on the fan and he put on this silly hat to go to sleep on till dawn.

November 15, 1993 Monday
Dear Diary,

Well I went to church and had a fun time anyhow I came home and chilled until waiting for Malcolm to come but um he wasn't home until around 8:30 and he decided to call so well I told him I'll come since you want to act silly about it. So when I got there Malcolm was looking cute as ever, well he had some nice looking suits very nice anyhow I was helping Malcolm match a tie with his suits and he always kept his neck hung to one side.

Well I asked why you keep hanging your head like that he didn't reply so well I continued to play around with the ties, but um he laid back and tried to fix my tie anyhow he laid down on the bed and begin telling me about a girl that he knew while at this time I felt a little scared thinking maybe it someone he wanted to be with or has been with. So well he told the girl he was studying and when he was getting ready to leave she wanted to hug him well she bit his neck which left a passion mark, I felt relieved because he really didn't have to tell me but I was happy about it I was reading the paper and listening to this certain song over and over again, well I was bothered with Malcolm's bumps on one side of his face well he was being very touchy so well I laid on my stomach and Malcolm begin kissing my back and neck and he tried to turn me over, but I wouldn't move so well I finally did and Malcolm was kissing and grinding all over me I enjoyed every feel of it. I care very deeply about my baby, so well before I knew it our clothes were coming off and well I was joking with Malcolm about if I leave my head turned this way you'll knock me off the bed so let get straight please, so well eager little Malcolm was on top of me and it felt so good to make love to my baby. Malcolm was kissing me a few minutes during the lovemaking then he got a little crazy later it was a little nutty, but the deeper he went in the better it felt. I never felt so good with anyone like Malcolm well

106

he finally came and well I was happy I swear I think Malcolm is slipping with the condom and shit because it felt like he came inside me, but I ignored it, well afterwards I had gotten dress and left.

December 8, 1993, Wednesday
Dear Diary,

I do love Malcolm very much; I feel the same feelings for him as I did for Robert he means so much to me. The night I spent with him he kept staring at me with this caring look on his face and eyes as he kept looking at me, I know Malcolm is having little more feelings than what he saying. Tonight I brought him a shirt with a pair of jeans to match; I think he has ties to go with it. I have to care about this guy to go out my way and buy him clothes. I've accomplish so much in the last year with Malcolm and I know he cares about me and I know I could count on him for anything, but holding out on me not having sex with me is not good now that I've fallen in love with him he means a lot to me.

Feb. 18, 1994 Friday
Dear Diary,

Well to begin my day I went to the clinic and took a pregnancy test to see whether I was, but the test came up negative thank goodness. Anyhow she presented some information on why we shouldn't have sex, which I felt like maybe a talk on how to prevent pregnancy instead.

After class I went to pay the electric place to get a copy of the bill and deposit the money that I wrote a few checks on. Lonnie and the crew we all went to see the movie Malice, which was really good, but later after we came home I felt upset and alone when I came back into the apartment I thought about Malcolm and ask him if he come over, he was hesitating at first about it, but gave in. He made it over about 45 minutes or better.

Malcolm was look cute as ever, we went back in my room and we talked and everything after explaining my problems he seems to understand and we had a nice time then I noticed he wanted to be playful, so it was getting late and I walked Malcolm to the door and I hugged him and told him he smells good. So I stood back and ask Malcolm would he shook me up with someone, he just looked at me and begin kissing and feeling down my pants and all of a sudden he picked me up and carried me to my room and I was all over him. So Malcolm asked did I have a condom and I told him in the drawer he pull it out and approached me and begin kissing and caressing me and begin inserting. I told him it was going to hurt, and he ask did it, I wanted to wait and I said no please continue he entered and it was painful at first, but felt so relaxing and good holding, kissing and feeling him.

After a few Moments of being in this position he sat up pulling me towards him which made me get on top of him, boy that's when I took over. I wanted to give Malcolm everything that I got, after so many accidents he chose to be behind it hurt and he couldn't stay in so well I laid back down and it hurt so bad maybe because I was dry and well Malcolm proceed and it hurt more and more he ask do you want me to stop and I told him no so well he took so long to come and the pain was getting more intense, finally he came. I was so happy and then he just lay on top of me and anyhow after we finish up and all Malcolm was getting dress and was ready to go so I kissed his ass goodbye.

April 9, 1994 Saturday
Dear Diary,

Hi well today has been a slow irritable day my stomach has been cramping up since like it was yesterday. I hate to go spend $8 to find out why my stomach has been cramping up like crazy.

Well as I sit here thinking about Malcolm and should I have enjoyed it as much as possible and not read too much into it. March 20th Malcolm and I took a trip to Wakulla Springs to enjoy the view, so I put on my daisy dukes in whom he thought I didn't have anything on, but he was very shock to see that I had on less than nothing. Well the trip there was no problem we enjoyed ourselves to the fullest. Malcolm later took us on a crazy ride, but it was okay.

May 16, 1994, Monday
Dear Diary,

Today was a nice day after taking Mom to work I decided to get some gas and mow the lawn up, well after doing that I took a shower dress and called around on some jobs and decided to look up a secretary job at Met. Blvd. After finding the place I called Malcolm to see what's up with him and well when I got there well he was in a silly mood I kept telling him to get off the computer so I can use it to put references on my resume and he just kept playing around. I begin smelling myself I said "Malcolm I need to buy a brand deodorant instead so well he stood up and was like messing with me until he smelled under my arms and was like you do smell as well. I decided to just kiss him instead, he was so into it we kissed and enjoyed it. Malcolm was feeling all over me rubbing my behind and face like it was nothing, we later sat on the chair he begin unbutton my dress and teasing at my breasts and well I felt a little uncomfortable after we fell over on the chair cause he saw my colorful panties so I begin to redress and well I sat down on the chair and well Malcolm came in front and he pulled me up by my hands and begin kissing me deeply again unbutton my dress and well I sat he grab my legs and pulled me up on his waist and I mention I weigh too much and um he held me up like that for a while, he sat down and begin kissing me and I was making the best of it that I can so I asked about the light he turned it off and went upstairs, when he returned he came and pulled my panties down and well it was on he felt so good very and always so well after a few times of that he let up and he came at that point I was feeling uncomfortable and was ready to go well after I dressed he was coming downstairs as nothing happened, after working on my resume I had to go.

May 20, 1994, Friday
Dear Diary,

Well work was pretty nice and it felt cool all day and well mama finally got her car back. I call Lonnie to take me to get my car. I later went back to the apartment feeling blue so I couldn't find anything in the kitchen so I call Malcolm and ask him could he bring me something to eat he kept beating around the bush so much till I was about to give up, but then he gave in and said he'll bring it.

After I hung up with Tim he call wanting to visit so I said fine and so he came over tripping and I got a little nervous and I kind of wanted to leave instead before Malcolm came up, so after he finally left 20 minutes later Malcolm approached look extra cute, he had the nerve to give me McDonald's of all things so I was like you know better than this so after tripping and over the food, we ate and so he begin tripping and wanted to be playful he was showing exercises and how he walks out, so after doing that he wanted to play because I wanted 50 cent well I had to play hard especially after he found his socks.

Well as I was doing earlier I notice how Malcolm kept pulling me to his hardness and rubbing up on him, he did this a lot so after look at Jamie Foxx and Arsenio Hall, I said "well Malcolm I guess it's time to go", and he said "in a minute" and at that I wanted to go to bed so I turned off the TV and the lights and climb into bed well he looked so unconcerned so well I climb on top of him and kiss him goodnight well he sat up and kiss me more aggressive and taking me to the fullest, rubbing and caressing my behind so well I grabbed him and hug him even more just being here.

Malcolm took off my garment and shorts and he picked me up and laid me on the bed and begin kissing caressing me in all the right areas. I was getting very into it as well so Malcolm begin undressing and asking about a condom and as he was putting it on I was getting very inpatient and he climbed on to me and put my legs in a crazy position and entered it hurt so bad and then he felt so delicious afterwards. I loved every Moment of it, so well he pulled me towards him to be on top so I could be in control. I was giving him everything until I felt this urge to use the bathroom and I couldn't hold it so I end up on my back it still felt weird, but he finally approaches his peak and all I wanted to do was just hold him instead he felt so warm and cuddly, after releasing he begin dressing and I put on my housecoat and walked Malcolm to the door and he gave me a hug and kiss goodnight.

May 25, 1994, Wednesday
Dear Diary,

Well today I went to Bainbridge to pay off my car debt and get my Car title back well after all that I went to grandma to just talk with her and see if she needed anything done around the house.

After work I went to the mall to get an outfit for Sunday and well I went home and called Malcolm and asked could he come over and well Malcolm did come with his cute self so well we moved all the furniture and well he was very hyper, so well he suggested we play ball together and I was like Okay I played well and we did have fun. So after that well he took me back to his apartment so but before that he went by the bank and withdraw some money and brought some Captain D's so his roommate was there and she was tripping about a class she was teaching so me and him was laughing about the Situation and well we looked at Jaws 2 and Arsenio afterwards so at five min to 12 we went to back to my place after I had took a bath so well me and Malcolm talked and I wanted him so bad I kept hugging him and rubbing against him wanting to go further, but he wouldn't he would never kiss me neither. He later mentioned he was going back on his word to stay focus and not have sex and retain a friendship instead. I was little taken back about this, but I had to respect his decisions even though I felt they were a little selfish say the least. After realizing nothing was going to happen I left.

August 1, 1994 Monday
Dear Diary,

Last night was an experience I never expected him to do. I called Malcolm from Shed's house just to see how he was doing and well he was tripping so after telling me he didn't want me over, I left Shed's and went home, but decided to turn around and go back to Malcolm anyway. I knock on is door to tell him good night (crazy huh), instead he told me to come and we immediately went to his room we talked for a Moment and I of course was getting annoyed with him, so I was excusing myself from him and started walking out the door telling him bye so then, he stood to the door and ask me to come back in I did and this time he paid more attention by listening to me, at this point my mind start drifting to other things especially look at Malcolm with those boxers on, they caused his penis to pop out and this happened numerous times until I just told him about it, he was a little embarrassed I kept laughing and teasing him about it until it look like he was getting upset. Malcolm grabbed my arm and ask me to apologize for laughing, I couldn't cause it was still funny to me then finally Malcolm silent my laughter by kissing my lips, ear and neck which were my hot spots. After our lovemaking session I had to go back to my world and just remember what happened last night and hope it's not the end.

CHAPTER 14

Missing my Friend

After this entry, it was the end. I was done with writing my emotional up and downs of my crazy life. Instead I begin to turn my attention to the series of events that happened afterwards. I was left drained and unfortunately alone. Later in that year I had a physical and emotional breakdown that caused me to reevaluate my life once again. I thought we were a couple, but I was sadly mistaken. The entries I wrote, talked mainly of our sexual moments and there were many, but in my mind with the love making being so intense why wouldn't I think otherwise, only to find out this was his way showing his affections, by paying attention to a woman's body and emotions. In all my experiences I've never had that type of relationship before. In my mind each time we had sex, it was making love. I felt embarrassed that I let my emotions get away from what was real to what wasn't.

Once I grab focus with my life, I reached out to Malcolm once again, but this time I knew what to expect from our relationship. He was my friend in more ways than one and just to reconnect with him was important to me as a whole I needed that. The Friendship I had with Malcolm was more therapeutic, being able to share more of myself and with him was amazing. I never had anyone to really listen to me, give advice and to feel for me. With Malcolm I was an opened book, to read and learn each page to figure Terri out and till this day, he's still finding pages that he missed.

My journey with Malcolm was totally different from my relationship with Robert; because with Malcolm I only wished he knew the struggles of what I endured in my teens and young adult life, maybe he wouldn't have taken our friendship to another level instead just left it "just Friends" and I should've have been honest with him in the beginning instead of longing for something more. Instead Malcolm represented what I should've waited for.

CHAPTER 15

Love at Last the Final Chapter

Our relationship didn't start off sweet and gentle as you may think. We needed a lot of repairs along the way. It was more like a roller coaster, when it first starts you can't believe your there in the moment and feeling *"OMG this is really happening"*, and once you reach the top, your heart start racing and you realize *OMG*, then close your eyes expecting that crazy feeling to happen. Once it descends, you think *"what a rush"*. That's how me and Malcolm were; we didn't know what to do once the ride was over.

The love I found with Malcolm was what I was looking for all my life, but mainly, it was a father figure. As a child, my father wasn't around and I had to learn the hard way about how to love, find someone to love me and I found all that in Malcolm.

Once I became pregnant with my first child, it was a scary feeling. One, we were both in school, Malcolm was completing his last year at Law school and me my second year at Keiser College, with that pressure why did I keep Devon. Second, I didn't know how Malcolm was going to react and if we were going to work, I knew Malcolm was a strong family man and I also knew our status from friend's w/ benefits to PARENTS will change the dynamics of our relationship completely.

Malcolm wasn't ready, nor was I even at 23. I was @ Keiser College completing my degree in Computer Science and Malcolm finishing up Law School, with that stress why keep him. I was afraid to even make the decision of letting Devon go. Feelings were all

During my pregnancy, it was a weird, exciting and difficult time all in one. I was 23 years old staying at home with my mom and sister and working a job that I didn't see a career in, that in itself would make any sane women crazy. Emotionally, I wanted what any pregnant women desires to have the father living and taking of us. I didn't have that luxury, because of our relationship and things were complicated. Malcolm and I tried to pulled through those 9 months which were hard, even after Devon's birth I had a time controlling my feelings when it came to him. I was a crazy, jealous, lunatic with a crazier mama, so with that I drove Malcolm further away than near.

My only defense was he was the father of my child and I wanted him and him only, but that wasn't our relationship. Even with all the craziness that took place we managed to expect another child. It took us a year or two to come back and focus on what was important; especially since baby #2 was on the way WOW *"yup 2 kids and not married, tell your mama & daddy that one and see what happens",*

We struggled for a moment to find a balance on staying together and working as a family, but I knew that was the only way of proving how important it was too me. When my baby girl turned 1 ½ we did what was needed to make our family a whole and finally got married.

CHAPTER 16

I's Married Now

Marriage is a different realm then shacking up. Once the rings are placed on your fingers, things change immediately. There's this person in front of you that you have vowed to love & cherish for the rest of your life, "the rest of my life WOW" to death do you part, those are amazing words but was I up for challenge to follow them.

That's the million dollar question we should ask ourselves before the wedding occurred. Instead we have no clue that he is or yourself for that matter, just let's have this beautiful wedding and let the rose's drop where they may, **NOT**. The first three years into our marriage was the worst, we couldn't communicate or meet half way to save our lives, I found more comfort with my friends and mama then I did with him, ain't that something. I hated where we lived but at the same time I had to go with my husband, we struggled a lot to keep it together and show a front, like all is well but behind closed doors it wasn't. I was more focus on changing him instead of just working with him.

Dear Diary

I always wanted to know the secret to my grandma's long marriage of 52 yrs, and she told me these three words; TALK, UNDERSTANDING AND MOSTLY PATIENCE and one thing she said was keep your marriage problems between you and your husband; in other words, don't invite others in that you can't look at again, once things are good.

There were times I wanted to call it quits, but I had my babies and they kept me there, after looking at our lives I realized I had to make changes. First, I had to stop listening to my **SINGLE** friends and my mama; they weren't providing the kind of advice to help my situation or their own, cause remember they are **SINGLE** for a reason. I realized at that moment only one person could help me, and it was GOD. I had to sit down and just PRAY about my life, marriage and family that was my secret to saving my family from separation.

One day, I woke up and said, "this is it, I'm going to learn to know my husband and let him know me", after that we begin to talk as a family, go to church as family and love as a family. This decision was important for me and my family. That's what most marriages, today lack, "making it work".

Once we became as one, a special miracle happened. We begin to notice our finances and family structure turn around and after 8 years together as man & wife, I became pregnant and had a beautiful baby boy. That pregnancy brought me and Malcolm closer than ever before. So many miracles happen around his birth. First, he wasn't in our plans and second, Peter was born on my brother in-law's birthday. It's amazing to watch GOD work and how this amazing gift brought peace and happiness at a time of sadness and heartbreak. GOD saw the change in us before we did, he just positioned us to find it and move forward and OMG we did, it was the best decision ever.

We begin to look for a bigger home to share our expanding family and to show my gratitude, I praise God for fulfilling my needs and desires to where I'm speechless sometimes. I can't tell you how truly blessed I am, to have the man of my dreams to be the father of my 3 beautiful babies. Malcolm, loves me dearly and I feel that love everyday even after all these years together.

I still find him attractive, whenever he walks into the room, all dressed up going or coming in from work, I get that school girl smile on my face, because he's mine. With this unexpected love that I've found, I can't imagine not having it.

Love is life and life is love and it's a beautiful thing. This is my visions of love found.

Thank you for reading my book. If you enjoyed it, please take a moment to leave me a review at your favorite retailer or Amazon.com?

Thanks!
S. A. Willis